TRILOGY NO. 105:
SMALLTOWN, U.S.A.
CAT JOHNSON

TRILOGY NO. 105: SMALLTOWN, U.S.A.

Published by Linden Bay Romance, 2006
Linden Bay Romance, LLC, U.S.
ISBN Trade paperback ISBN # 1-905393-96-2
ISBN MS Reader (LIT) ISBN # 1-905393-95-4
Other available formats (no ISBNs are assigned):
PDF, PRC & HTML

Cover art by *Beverly Maxwell*

First, a confession…I am a kept woman.

This book is dedicated to the man who pays the bills, allowing me the luxury of following my dream. (Get your mind out of the gutter, he's my husband.)

THE HORSEMAN

Chapter 1

Jared Gordon considered himself a lucky man.

He had a steaming hot mug of coffee and a piece of mile-high lemon meringue pie in front of him. The diner's AC unit pumped cool air out of the vent just above him, allowing him to forget the beastly southern summer heat outdoors. And one of his best friends, who also happened to be the deputy sheriff, which was handy in case he ever got into trouble, sat directly opposite him.

Life, he decided, was good. Until, he saw *her* walk in the door.

"Aww, shit." Jared slumped down in his seat and shielded his eyes with one hand.

Bobby Barton glanced up from his own plate of apple crisp à la mode and smirked. "You brought that one on yourself, kiddo."

Just what Jared needed from his friend at this moment in time, an 'I told you so'.

"Oh, shut up," he hissed.

Bobby continued smiling and shook his head knowingly. "You can take it out on me all you want. But you know damn well I warned you off of her. She wants a wedding ring on her finger in the worst way. Hookin' a successful horseman like yourself would have been right up her alley."

Jared risked a glance at Sue Ann, the woman in question, as she sashayed her shapely hips over to the counter. Those hips had been his downfall to begin with. Sleeping with her was a risk he should never have taken, just like daring to sneak a look at her now. He was punished for both by a wicked glare over her shoulder before she leaned in and started whispering with Misty, the waitress behind the counter. From the way they both looked at him, it was pretty obvious what the topic of conversation was.

He groaned and Bobby laughed again.

"This town is too small, Jared. You can't go fishin' in the local pond if you're only going to throw your catch back after you're through with it."

"She agreed it was just a casual thing. Just two adults scratchin' an itch every once in a while," Jared defended himself.

That elicited a rude noise from Bobby. "Yeah, right. Jared, what women say and what they mean are usually the exact opposite, in my experience. You better stick to horses, at least you know somethin' about them."

"Hey, I knew enough to get the hell out of there when she started hinting marriage." Jared wasn't a complete idiot. He simply hadn't anticipated her reaction to his 'maybe we should just be friends' speech. Bobby was right; Pigeon Hollow was a small town, way too small.

"You were lucky. I wouldn't put it past that one to try *anything* to snag herself a hubby." Bobby raised a brow knowingly while bobbing his head with a wisdom-filled nod.

"Oh, no. I'm too smart for that. She kept tellin' me she was on the pill, but I still took care of things myself. With two older brothers, that message has been drilled into my head since before I hit puberty."

Bobby looked impressed. "Good to hear. How are Jack and Jimmy, anyway?"

"They're back at the base, happily protectin' the country from the bad guys. They call a couple of times a week. It keeps Mama happy. She misses them a lot."

"And you don't?" Bobby looked skeptical.

"Yeah, I do. It was nice havin' them both home for a while." Jack and Jimmy were both in the military, so they had to live at the base. When they'd been home on leave recently, it made Jared realize how much he missed having his brothers around. At least he still had his good old friend Bobby.

"Well, do me a favor. Next time they're comin' home for a visit, can you give me some notice? It seems trouble follows those two around."

Jared had often thought that himself. He laughed. "You got it."

He watched Sue Ann still chatting up the waitress and wondered if he ever dared eat here again. Since this was the only diner around for miles, his choices were pretty limited. Of a more immediate concern, he figured the chances of getting a refill on his java today were slim to none.

Glancing into his near empty mug, Jared looked up at Bobby. "What day does your sister Lizzie waitress here?"

Bobby frowned and asked deeply and slowly, "Why?" He was very protective of his little sister.

Jared couldn't really blame him; Lizzie Barton was the single mother of a nine-year-old son. Jared also knew—hell, everybody did—that there was a bit of history between the Bartons and the Gordons. His brother Jack and Bobby's other sister, Mary Sue, had had some wild times back in high school. But she was not the sister in question here, and as far as Jared knew, no Gordon man had ever messed with Lizzie Barton.

"Relax. Jeez, Bobby. You know she's like a sister to me, too. I just figure it may not be safe to come here for a while unless Lizzie serves me since you-know-who is so chummy with the other waitress." Jared kept his voice low and cocked a head in the direction of Sue Ann. She turned from the counter and walked past their table with a withering glare.

Bobby's face broke out into a grin again, which was as bad as an 'I told you so', maybe worse. Bobby's eyes followed Sue Ann out the door and then he said, "Be afraid, Jared. Be very afraid."

Jared rolled his eyes. "Thanks a lot. You're so helpful."

Bobby scooped the last of his pie into his mouth, slurped one more sip of coffee and stood. Digging into his pocket, he threw some cash on the table. "If it's safe to leave you unprotected from the woman scorned, I have to get back to work now."

Jared scowled. As if Bobby didn't take hour-long coffee breaks all day long! But actually, he should get back to the farm himself. He nodded, finishing the last of his own pie. "All right." He longed for another sip of hot coffee to go

3

with the last few bites of pie. "Check on Lizzie's schedule for me," he added.

He heard Bobby laughing as the door swung shut behind him.

Jared threw some money on the table and was about to leave when he thought better of it. He wouldn't put it past Misty, as one of Sue Ann's friends, to accuse him of not paying his check. You never knew what a woman would do for another woman to get back at a man. It was practically a global conspiracy.

He gathered up the check, Bobby's cash and his own, and carried it up to the cash register. What had this world come to that a man couldn't enjoy his pie in peace without fear of retribution?

Jared had been so entranced in his paranoia over Sue Ann, that he'd failed to notice the stranger who now stood at the counter, tapping her foot like a jack hammer against the faded linoleum floor.

He raised a brow with interest. They didn't get many strangers in town. By the looks of her, she didn't come from any of the towns nearby, either. Firstly, she was dressed in a suit, long-sleeved jacket and all, in spite of the summer heat. She was someone who usually spent her days in an air-conditioned office somewhere. He could tell. Secondly, she was so impatient she was practically vibrating. Locals knew things moved slowly in the south, especially in the heat of the summer.

The stranger was huffing and puffing and shooting dagger-filled looks at the waitress, who bussed his table while she ignored them both at the counter. Jared was the reason they were being ignored, so he did feel a bit responsible. Being a southern gentleman, born and bred, he decided to step in and help the stranger in need.

"What do ya' need, darlin'?"

She spun to look at him. "You work here?"

"No, but I'll yell to Mac back there. He'll get it for you." The owner of the diner was in the kitchen, cooking. Jared

4

could see him through the opening in the wall.

She glanced one more time at the waitress who still hadn't acknowledged their presence. "All I want is a cup of coffee to go. And since I haven't seen a Starbucks anywhere, I'd hoped I could get one here."

Thinking that more caffeine was probably the last thing this tightly strung babe needed, Jared nodded. "You surely can. Best coffee in town." He didn't add that it was also practically the only coffee in town, if you didn't count the McDonald's. Fast-food coffee didn't appeal to him. He liked a real mug that a man could wrap his hand around. Come to think of it, those were the qualities he looked for in a woman, too.

He leaned over the counter and called out, "Hey, Mac. This little lady here wants a coffee to go."

"Where's Misty?" Mac growled from the back, looking mighty hot and cranky in the kitchen.

Jared glanced at the waitress and decided not to dig his own grave any deeper. "She's busy."

Mac grumbled his way to the front and poured coffee into a to-go cup, shoving a plastic lid, the cream and the sugar at her.

As citified and impatient as she'd seemed at first, Mac's gruffness even put the stranger on her best behavior. "Thank you so much. How much do I owe you?" she asked sweetly.

"Just the coffee?" Mac asked.

"The coffee and directions, if you wouldn't mind."

"Coffee is seventy-five. Directions are free." Jared watched as even gruff Mac started to warm up to her. He had to admit, she was a looker, in a perfect, polished, city sort of way. Sleek blonde hair, cut in what he supposed was a fashionable style. Pretty blue eyes. Perfect nails painted in pale pink with the white edges showing.

"Seventy-five cents?" She looked surprised. Jared noticed she had four single dollar bills in her hand. Four dollars for one cup of coffee? She was definitely a city person. She put one bill down on the counter and pushed it toward Mac. "Keep the change."

"Thanks. Now where do you need to go?" Mac shoved the money in the register. Jared took that opportunity to slide his own bill and cash onto the counter, but his hand stopped dead for a second when he heard the woman say, "Gordon Equine? It's a horse farm. Do you know it?"

Mac raised a brow and glanced sideways at Jared. "Sure do. And what business do you have with the Gordons, pretty lady? You in the market for a stud?"

Now it was her turn to raise a brow. She pursed her lips, as if considering. "Perhaps."

Mac laughed boisterously in his gruff voice and cocked his head in Jared's direction. "This here fella' can give you directions. I got something on the stove."

Hmm. What could this tough cookie from the city want with him?

He decided not to tip his hand just yet. Jared gave her directions all right, the long way to the farm, which would give him just enough time to arrive right before her.

Sure, it was juvenile. But hell, you had to make your own entertainment around Pigeon Hollow. Who better to make it with than a pretty blonde stranger who might possibly be in the market for a Gordon stud?

Chapter 2

Mandy Morris got into her rental car, which had gotten hellishly hot during the few minutes she'd been in the diner. Turning on the ignition, she flipped the AC on high.

Her coffee securely in the cup holder, she grabbed her pad and pencil from the passenger seat and started scribbling. She spoke aloud to herself as she wrote. "Pigeon Hollow. Interesting characters: Cook at diner (Mac), Cutie that gave directions (need to investigate him further)."

She laid the pad back on the seat next to her so it would be accessible in case an idea came to her while she was driving, then gripped her coffee and took a sip. Not bad for seventy-five cents. Humph! What a difference from Los Angeles. You couldn't get the empty cup in LA for seventy-five cents, forget about the coffee inside!

She shook her head and zipped the car easily out of the parking space, onto the main road through town. You couldn't drive anywhere in LA without getting bogged down in traffic, either. Pigeon Hollow, the quintessential small town, was proving to be a nice change, in many ways.

On Main Street (yes, that was the actual name) an antique-looking spinning red, white and blue pole announced the local barbershop. A little further down, Mandy spotted a salon. If she did get stuck there for any length of time, at least she could get her nails done.

On the outskirts of town, she saw a typical small town honky-tonk bar, neon beer signs and all. And right next door, conveniently located for both drunks and lovers, was The Hideaway Motel. She supposed if she decided to stay, this would be her only option for lodging. That was a bit frightening. Judging by the looks of it, The Beverly Hills Hotel it wasn't. Oh, well. If it was really horrible, she could just get drunk next door and then pass out, oblivious to any horrors the room may hold.

Pushing that thought out of her mind, she concentrated on remembering the directions to the horse farm and prepared herself for what she might find there. Hopefully the owner would at least have those all-important front teeth and be able to speak coherent English. If not, she'd deal with that somehow, too.

She smiled when she remembered the joke Mac had made back at the diner. She was in the market for a stud all right. The question was, would luck be on her side and provide one for her in the guise of one of the horsemen at Gordon Equine? Her career might depend upon it.

~

Jared sped his truck up the magnolia-lined driveway of his mother's farm and skidded to a stop in the gravel. He flew out the door and ran for the barns. Seeing his two hired hands inside, he instructed them breathlessly, "There's a cute blonde in a suit on her way here. Don't tell her who I am. Got it?"

Raul and Mick both looked at him as of he were crazy but nodded.

Jared nodded in response and went back outside to decide where to wait for the nameless over-caffeinated woman.

He'd settled himself in what he thought of as a casual pose, leaning back against the corral fence with one boot hooked on the bottom rail and his arms crossing his chest, when her car pulled slowly up the drive. She parked and got out. Still wearing the suit jacket, in spite of the heat, she looked around from behind a pair of dark sunglasses.

He knew the moment she spotted him, sunglasses or not. She was perfectly still for a second, and then made her way toward him, maneuvering the high heels gingerly through the gravel. She looked so out of place, he couldn't help but smile. What in the world was she doing here in Pigeon Hollow and, more importantly, at his farm?

Slipping her glasses on to the top of her head, she looked up to talk to him, since she was a good head shorter than his own six feet, even with her heels. As she laid one hand on the top rail of the fence, he watched her fingers drum away against the wood. This woman was a constant ball of motion.

"So, if you were coming here anyway, why didn't you just let me follow you? Or *weren't* you coming here anyway?"

He smirked. "Are you accusing me of followin' you, little lady?"

"Yes, I think I am."

He smiled broader. "Well don't get yourself all in a tizzy. I work here."

"Why didn't you say that back at the diner?"

Jared shrugged. "What fun would that be?"

She let out a short laugh. "Maybe you should get cable TV. You wouldn't have to work so hard to entertain yourself."

She blew out a breath and ran a hand along the back of her neck and under her shoulder length hair. She was looking mighty warm in that jacket, and he was starting to sweat in sympathy. Then she took the jacket off.

That was enough to make a man stand up and take notice. Now, she looked downright hot. He was sweating for real now, and not from the heat. Under that jacket, she was wearing nothing but a tight, low-cut, sleeveless top. Much better, he decided, forcing his eyes up from her breasts and back to her face.

"We've got satellite TV, but a pretty stranger is much more entertainin'." He treated her to his most charming smile.

She was pursing her lips, as if trying not to smile, when she said, "I need to speak with the owner. Do you think you could stop whatever you are doing…" She looked around pointedly to let him know she didn't think he was doing much of anything, which was true. Then she continued. "…and go and get her for me?"

That perked up Jared's ears. "Her? What makes you think the owner is a 'her'?"

"I do my research," she answered simply.

"And?" The question of why she was researching them

9

remained.

"*And*, I know that this farm is registered with the small business bureau as being a woman-owned business."

He raised a brow, about to interrogate her further, when the woman owner in question, his mama, stuck her head out of the kitchen door and called for him. "Jared, honey. I need your expenses from last month, and the computer crashed again."

Now it was the stranger's turn to raise a skeptical brow, and the look she gave him was full of suggestion. "Is that the owner?"

He started walking toward the kitchen, resigned to the fact that the nosy but hot stranger was bound to follow. "Yup."

As anticipated, she practically jogged to keep up with him. "Are you and she…ah, you know?"

He stopped dead and turned to look at her with horror. "No!"

She shrugged. "It's OK, I'm just wondering."

Jared shot her another horrified look and then scowled all the way to the back door at that lewd suggestion. But then he took a moment to re-evaluate his mother the way a stranger might see her. She had been really, really young when she got married and started having babies. She had just turned fifty, but she took good care of herself. Dressed in cut-off jeans and flip-flops the way she was today, she looked easily in her forties. Jared was in his late twenties. He knew there were some actresses in Hollywood who dated guys twenty years younger, but still, yuck! She was his mama!

He shook his head. This woman came from a totally different world, one Jared could barely comprehend. Given that, he tried not to judge her as a pervert, particularly since he had kept his real identity from her. And he resolved to find out her damn name so he could stop thinking of her as 'this woman'.

He held the screen door open for her, allowing her to

walk through first and then walked over to his mama. Hell, he was raised right, he knew how to act around a lady, even if she was a salesman, uh, person. He would have introduced them, but again, he didn't know the woman's name. Luckily, she was one of those assertive business-like types and stepped right up without waiting for him. "Ms. Lois Gordon?"

His mama nodded.

"I'm Mandy Morris." She smiled and stuck out her hand. "It's a pleasure to meet you."

Mama smiled and shook her hand. "The pleasure is all mine. Jared never brings his girls to meet me."

Mandy—cute name—glanced at him briefly and then turned back to his mother. She smiled. "I'm sorry, Ms. Gordon. I think you've gotten the wrong impression. I'm not one of Jared's 'girls'. I'm actually here to see you. I have a business proposition for you. If you have some time now, I'd love to discuss it with you privately."

Jared noticed she said the last word to very pointedly let him know he was not welcome to participate in the discussion about whatever this business proposal was. He looked her over again. No way was she here to make an offer to buy the farm, or even a horse. She was probably trying to sell them ad space in the local yellow pages or something.

His mama, sweet as ever, said, "Ms. Morris. I may be the owner on record for Gordon Equine, but my son runs the farm. All I do nowadays is handle the paperwork and the accounting and crash the computer." Mama smiled and indicated the computer, phone and stack of papers on a desk set up in the corner of the kitchen.

She insisted on working in the kitchen rather than making one of the many other rooms into an office because she was usually cooking or baking something at the same time she was working on the books. Multi-tasking, isn't that what they called it today?

Mandy looked surprised. "Your son?" She shot him quite a nasty look. Uh, oh. Now he was in for it for withholding that apparently important information.

Mama smiled at him. "Uh, huh. Jared's my youngest."

"Your youngest?" she squeaked. Again with the surprise.

Mama nodded.

"I'm sorry. You, ah, just look too young to have older children."

Mama laughed and shrugged. "Darlin', all a woman needs in life is good face cream and a proper bra, but thank you anyway. I have to tell you, though, flattery won't get me to buy whatever you're sellin', Ms. Morris."

Mandy shook her head and smiled. "I'm not flattering you. And I'm not selling anything. I'm a television producer from California. I've been on the road for two weeks, visiting potential towns for a new reality series about small towns in America. If you agree, I think my search is over. I want you, Ms. Gordon, and your son Jared, and even Mac the cook from the diner. And the honky tonk, and the barbershop...even The Hideaway Motel. I love this entire town. With your help, we'll have a smash hit on our hands, as big as *Survivor* or *American Idol*. We'll put Pigeon Hollow on the map!"

Jared had stood quietly for her entire crazy revelation. He finally broke his gaze away from Mandy and glanced at Mama. She was looking uncertainly back at him.

"Let me explain a bit about how it will work. I'll have a few camera crews around town focusing on the key characters in town as well as the hotspots. Of course I'd have a camera on Jared and you here at the farm. One in the diner, that seems like a hot spot, and Mac is a great character. I don't think we'll need the crews here filming while you're both sleeping, but the camera will be rolling every moment you're awake."

Every moment he was awake? Jared had heard enough. He stepped forward. "Ms. Morris."

She interrupted him. "Please, call me Mandy."

He wondered if she'd be so sweet when they said no to

12

this insanity. "Mandy. I'd like to discuss this alone with my mother. If you don't mind, maybe you could wait in the livin' room?" He laid a gentle hand on her elbow. She nodded, but looked confused, like she couldn't imagine they wouldn't jump at this opportunity.

When he finally had Mandy settled in the other room with the glass of iced tea Mama had insisted she take, he joined his mother back in the kitchen. "Mama. This is crazy. I don't want cameras all over the farm! And have you seen any of those shows? They cut and edit the tapes to make folks look however the producers choose."

"It would be good advertising," Mama reasoned.

"Advertising? For god's sake, Mama. Who the hell in the audience of this crap show is goin' to be in the market to buy a champion-bred horse?"

"Jared Gordon, you watch your mouth. We may be partners in this business, but I am still your mother. You don't use that kind of language or that tone in my house."

Jared hung his head and took a deep calming breath. "I'm sorry. This all took me by surprise. I thought she was sellin' somethin'. I never imagined this."

"Jared, darlin'." His mama laid a hand on his arm. "You run the farm, and you will be the one most affected if we do this. If you say no, then it's no. That's fine by me."

He looked at her closely, trying to evaluate what she was really feeling. "You sure?"

She nodded. "Yup. The decision is up to you. But *you* have to tell her." Mama smiled and walked back to the computer.

Jared groaned and headed for the living room. He had a feeling she wasn't going to take rejection well.

~

Mandy placed her iced tea back down on the coaster and glanced absently around the living room, planning camera shots in her mind. The room looked like it was probably used a few times a year for company, or when the family needed to stash away a television producer while they

13

discussed her.

It was a nice enough room, but there was no heart in it. The kitchen was the heart of this home. She could tell that the moment she walked in. A freshly baked pie sat on the counter. The centerpiece of the kitchen, the charming, worn wooden table, looked as if it had been there for more than a century. Mandy could picture the lady of the house, still an extremely attractive woman, running the family business from the kitchen computer while baking pies.

She smiled when she remembered Lois' philosophy on aging well. *Good face cream and a proper bra.* Part homemaker, part corporate mogul, Lois Gordon was a down-to-earth, likeable version of Martha Stewart, with a sense of humor to boot! Not to mention one sizzling hot, ratings-grabbing son.

They'd have to shoot Jared in his blue jeans and cowboy boots, perhaps sweaty and shirtless. She pictured him looking meltingly handsome on tape. A solid block of muscular manliness. The golden highlights in his brown hair glinting in the sun. His hazel eyes smoldering at the camera. What viewer wouldn't love the man and his horses?

Mandy could almost feel the weight of the Emmy award in her hand. *Best prime time reality series…*

Her reverie was interrupted as she watched Jared stroll into the living room. He sat on the couch opposite her chair and rested his muscular forearms on his knees as he leaned forward towards her. "Ms. Morris…"

"Mandy," she corrected.

He nodded once. "Mandy. We're gonna have to take a pass on your offer."

"Excuse me?"

He shrugged. "It's just not for us. I'm sorry."

She shook her head in disbelief. "I don't know why you would want to pass up this opportunity. Perhaps you and your mother don't understand what I'm offering…"

"We do, but the answer is still no."

Mandy was not used to anyone actually saying no to her.

Particularly not men. She shook her head, speechless.

Jared laughed. "You look…shocked."

"Honestly, I am."

"I'm sure you'll find another town that you love just as much as Pigeon Hollow. Small towns like this are a dime a dozen in the south."

The town maybe, but not a woman-owned horse farm, and a handsome horseman with a voice like silk to go with it.

Mandy dug a business card out of the pocket of the suit jacket folded in her lap, stood and handed it to him. "Look. I'm not giving up. I have one other town to see just south of here and then I'm coming back. I hope you'll have reconsidered and have a different answer for me when I do."

He treated her to a gorgeous crooked smile. "I'm not gonna say that I wouldn't be happy to see you again, pretty lady. But my answer's not gonna change."

She felt her heart quicken just a bit. Was he flirting with her? She was not at all opposed to a bit of flirtation with a handsome man, particularly if it got her a signed consent form and a hit show in the end. She might actually enjoy a bit of innocent gentlemanly male attention. It would be a nice change from the lecherous men in LA.

Catching his eye, she said, "I respect your decision. But I'd still like to stop by on my way back through. If that's OK."

She watched Jared study her closely before saying, "Sure."

Mandy felt his eyes on her back as she walked out the door and smiled. She wasn't giving up yet.

Chapter 3

Two days later, Mandy drove down Main Street in Pigeon Hollow and fell in love with it all over again. The other town she'd gone to visit had been a bust. But then again, no town was going to live up to this one since she had set her sights on it. So now, it was two days later and she was still without a town for her show. Unless she could somehow change Jared's mind.

She slowed as she neared the diner and spotted a white pickup truck with *Gordon Equine* painted on the door. She might be in luck. After finding a parking spot, she pulled the jacket off and smoothed the short sleeveless sundress. Keeping Lois Gordon's advice in mind, she hiked her boobs up a bit higher in her bra and was happy with the resulting cleavage. A bit more lipstick and she was good to go.

She walked into the diner and got a blast full of welcome, air-conditioned cold air in the face. Raising her sunglasses up and setting them on top of her head, she glanced around the diner. But Jared wasn't anywhere to be seen. Maybe he was in the restroom?

A cup of seventy-five cent coffee at the counter would give her time to wait for him without looking suspicious, and she could get a look at some of the other local characters while she was at it.

Slipping onto one of the high counter stools, she ordered a coffee and then turned her attention to the dark-haired man in the khaki uniform next to her. A small town sheriff, with a star on his chest and all. And he was cute, too. God, she had to tape the show in this town. It was too perfect. She couldn't have made it any better if she cast it herself!

Just to prove her already lofty opinion of the town's characters and their marketability, Mac spotted her and called out from the kitchen, "Hey there, pretty lady. You come back for your stud?"

She laughed and decided to play along with the joke. If she was going to flirt her way into a contract, she might as well start now. "Actually, I did. But even though I saw his truck outside, he doesn't seem to be in here."

At her response, Mac's laughter filled the kitchen and spilled out into the diner making the few patrons inside look up. Even the hunky sheriff turned his ice blue eyes to look at her.

"You talkin' about the Gordon truck outside?"

She nodded. "I was looking for Jared Gordon."

He raised an inquisitive brow at that. "Were you now?"

"Uh, huh. Know him?" She was getting good at this southern speak. Short, sweet and to the point.

"I might."

She smiled. "Either you do or you don't."

He watched her closely. "You're not from around here."

It wasn't a question, but she answered it anyway. "No, I'm not."

"What you want with him?" Mr. Personality asked her.

She shook her head and let out a short laugh. "You southerners sure are suspicious. I thought you were supposed to be famous for your hospitality. The kindness of strangers and all that."

He shrugged. "We watch out for our own."

She'd give anything for a camera right now. It was just too perfect. *We watch out for our own, stranger.* She wouldn't have been at all surprised if John Wayne swaggered through the door and spit some tobacco on the floor. Well, maybe a little surprised, since he was dead, but the entire town had the feel of a place out of its time.

"You got much crime around here, Sheriff?" She had to know more, she couldn't help herself. She could put a camera in the car with him all during his shift. It would be amazing. Although, if she thought Jared was going to be a tough sell, this guy would probably be worse, by the looks of him. He hadn't even cracked a smile. And forget about flirting with him, she'd probably get locked up in the town jail for solicitation or something.

"Deputy."

"Excuse me?"

"I'm a deputy, not the sheriff."

"*The* sheriff. You mean there's only one?" She had visions of sheriff Andy Griffith and his deputy Barney Fife in small town Mayberry back in the black and white days of TV during the sixties.

He frowned at her as if he thought she was an imbecile. "'Course there's only one."

"Of course. Sorry."

Still looking suspiciously at her, he threw a few dollars down on the counter, inclined his head to her in a kind of goodbye gesture and strode his booted feet right out of the diner.

But the fun wasn't over for Mandy yet. Just as 'I'm a deputy' left, the waitress came over to her. "You lookin' for Jared Gordon?"

Mandy looked the chubby young woman up and down. Her nametag read *Misty*. How sweet. "Yes, Misty. I am."

"You, uh, *dating* him?"

She'd used the word 'dating' like it was a euphemism for something else, a word that wasn't quite so nice and would get you an FCC fine if you used it on network TV. Well, well, well. Was this jealousy she saw before her? The plot thickened.

"No, I'm not. Are you?"

The brunette shook her head, sending the ponytail held back with the unfashionably large hair accessory flying from side to side. "Nope. But my friend is. And she wouldn't take kindly to no woman snoopin' around Jared."

Hmmm. What was this? A warning? A threat? And why the hell was she suddenly feeling jealous herself that Jared had a girlfriend? Or at least a girl he was 'dating'. She supposed she could take solace in the fact that he'd never brought whoever this girl was home to meet his mother, from what Lois had said.

"I'm not 'snooping'. I have business with Gordon Equine."

"What kind of business? You ain't lookin' like no horsewoman to me."

Mandy had had about enough of the waitress and her grammatically incorrect interrogation. "*Private* business. Thanks for the coffee."

She dug a dollar bill out of her purse and shoved it beneath the coffee cup, still feeling like she was committing robbery by paying only a dollar with tip for a cup of coffee.

Mandy stood, called a goodbye to Mac in the back and was out the door, enjoying a bit too much the fact that she'd left the waitress suspicious as to her intentions toward Jared. Good, it would serve that Misty right for being so nosy.

Still not knowing why there was a Gordon truck parked outside and no Gordon inside, she decided to head over to the farm. She had to talk to Jared, or at least his mother. This town was too intertwined to film here if she didn't have all of the main characters on board. And as far as she was concerned, the Gordons struck her as the town headliners.

At the farm, she found Lois Gordon where else but in the kitchen, pulling a pie out of the oven. She looked adorable in capri jeans and a button down shirt tied at the waist.

"Hey, there, darlin'!"

She smiled. "Hi, Mrs. Gordon."

"Lois."

She nodded. "Lois. Do you bake a pie everyday?"

Lois smiled and pulled off her oven mitts. "Pretty much. Jared and the boys who work for us enjoy it. But this pie is for my book club meeting tonight. Sorry I can't offer you a piece. I've got some fresh lemonade made though."

Mandy held up a hand. "That's fine. Thank you anyway."

"What can I do for you, darlin'?"

"I was just wondering if you'd thought any more about the show. I really think you'd be great."

Lois sat down and patted the seat next to her. Mandy lowered herself into it. "Darlin', that decision isn't mine to make. It's Jared's. More than half the responsibility of

19

working this farm is already his, but all of it will be when I'm gone. I have to respect his decision."

Mandy smiled and fingered a small crack in the old table. "I don't think you're going anywhere for a long time."

"From your mouth to God's ears. But nobody knows what's in store for them."

Mandy breathed deep. "I just don't know why he's so against it."

Lois shrugged. "He can be stubborn." She let out a short laugh. "That's a Gordon trait, I'm afraid. But in any case, you'll have to talk to him yourself."

Mandy pursed her lips. "I tried. The truck was at the diner, but I didn't see Jared."

Lois shook her head. "The boys borrowed the truck to go into town. Jared's out back behind the barn, unloading the hay truck."

Mandy sat up straighter in her chair. "Really?"

Lois looked at her and smiled. She nodded. "Really. You can go on back and see him, if you want."

Mandy jumped up. "OK, I will. Thanks."

"I'll be seeing you, Mandy."

Mandy paused in the kitchen doorway. "I hope so, but if Jared doesn't agree, I'll be leaving for LA tomorrow."

Lois just smiled. "I think I'll be seeing more of you."

~

Standing on a mountain of tightly stacked hay bales, Jared flung another two from his perch atop the trailer into the small door high up in the wall of the barn. He pulled his shirt off and wiped the sweat from his face with it. If he had known his hay guy was going to drop the trailer off today, he would never have let Raul and Mick both go into town to pick up horse feed. And since it was lunchtime, they'd probably stopped at the diner, too, so he couldn't expect them back for a while.

He huffed out a breath. He would throw the hay in, but they could have the pleasure of stacking the two hundred plus bales inside the hay room when they got back. That thought helped a bit, but not much. He adjusted his gloves, grabbed the string of two more bales, one in each hand, and heaved them through the door.

"Hey! Casanova!"

Jared smiled when he heard Bobby's voice from below. "Bobby! You're just in time to help."

"Are you crazy? I joined the department so I wouldn't have to be a farmer. Too much damn work."

"You're telling me," Jared grumbled. "And why are you calling me Casanova?"

"You know why a cute blonde in expensive clothes would be asking about you at the diner?"

Jared broke out in a grin. "She was? Hot damn!"

"So you do know her."

"Oh, yeah. Not near well enough, but I know her."

"All right, that's all I wanted to know. I'll be on my way then before you figure out a way to make me help."

Jared laughed. "That's OK. With the news you just brought, I'll give you a reprieve from helping this one time."

Bobby raised a brow, considering. "I think I might rather hear what happens when she finally finds you."

"Well, that's gonna cost you because hopefully it's gonna be one hell of a story! At least a full hay truck worth of help, maybe two."

Bobby laughed. "I'll have to think about that. I'm still on duty, I'll see you tonight at the bar."

Resisting the urge to drive into town right then, Jared sincerely hoped Mandy did find him soon and that he'd have something worthwhile to tell Bobby about when he met him later tonight. At least now he had something good to occupy his mind while he finished unloading the truck. He grabbed another two bales and hefted them into the barn.

Turning to reposition himself, he saw a sight that was even better than his imagination. The pretty little thing herself was walking toward him as if she was tiptoeing through a minefield.

"I'll have to remember not to wear my best shoes when I

come here," she announced, shading her eyes with her hand as she looked up at him.

"It sounds like you plan on coming here often, pretty lady." He grinned. That was fine by him.

"You agree to do the show and I'll be seeing you every day for eight weeks."

Hmmm. Tempting and disappointing at the same time. "Darlin', if that's the only reason you're here, I'm afraid you wasted your time." Of course that was it. She wanted to see him about the damn show. Too bad. He'd hoped she was interested in more than just that.

She smiled up at him sweetly. "Can't blame a girl for trying. But no, that's not the only reason I'm here."

Well, now they were getting somewhere. He dropped down to the ground next to her and leaned against the bed of the trailer. He watched her eyes drop to his bare chest before she finally raised them back to his face. Very interesting. "Why are you here, then?" he asked.

"Well, I'm not really sure anymore. You see, on my way over here to see you, I met a friend of your girlfriend's at the diner and she pretty much told me to stay away from you. Do you have a girlfriend in town, Jared?"

"No." That just figured. One indiscretion—all right, three month's worth of indiscretions—with Sue Ann and she was going to try to ruin his life forever.

"The waitress thinks you do."

"The waitress is wrong."

Mandy watched him closely for a moment and then said, "I've got a room at The Hideaway." She rolled her eyes. "Heaven help me, I'll be staying there until I leave for LA tomorrow. I just wanted to let you know."

He was just snickering at her low opinion of their local motel, not that he blamed her, when she turned to go. He put a hand on her arm and stopped her. "That's it?"

She turned back. "That's all I've got to say. Do you have anything more to say?"

This girl wasn't going to make it easy on him, was she?

First she tells him where she's staying, and then she's leaving? Talk about mixed signals. Things were just too damn confusing when women were in charge of them. He'd have to take control and get them back on track.

"I'm gonna be at the bar right next to The Hideaway tonight. I'm meetin' a friend there," he informed her.

"A friend?" She raised a brow.

He laughed. As if he would invite her to come if he was meeting a girl there. "A guy friend. Why don't you walk over and join us there. Around eight."

"Maybe, if I'm not too busy." Then she turned again and left with a satisfied smile on her lips.

He shook his head and watched her go. She was definitely one high-maintenance chick. She was going to make him work for it, all right. Why did that realization make her even more appealing?

He shook his head at himself and climbed back up onto the hay truck, with a whole lot more to think about now.

Chapter 4

Mandy drove back into town without even really seeing the road ahead of her. She couldn't get out of her head the vision of Jared, half naked and throwing hay bales, two at a time like they weighed nothing.

Two good things had come out of their little meeting amid the hay. First, he had invited her to meet him and a friend out at the bar tonight. Not exactly a date, but it was a start. Second, and even more importantly, he had confirmed her suspicion—or was it hope—that he didn't have a girlfriend. But there was definitely a story there, and she'd get to the bottom of it somehow. Jealous exes and pissed off women made for great television.

Of course she was going to be at that bar tonight, even though she had pretended she was only considering it. Hell or high water wouldn't keep her away. If she couldn't convince a small-town guy who was already attracted to her to sign the consent form for the show while under the influence of alcohol, then she had better hang up her producer hat. Really, if she couldn't handle the folks here in Pigeon Hollow, forget about the sharks in LA.

Mandy did some errands in town. Soaked up some more of the local culture. Made more notes. She'd finally killed all the time she could and headed back to the motel.

The Hideaway loomed before the hood of the rental car as she pulled up to her room door. It really wasn't that bad. She'd been pleasantly surprised upon check in. There was no visible grime or bugs. The furnishings in the good-sized space, though worn and unfashionable, were at least neat and clean. The housekeeping was decent, so she wouldn't have to wear rubber shoes to shower in or anything like that. There was even a hookup for her laptop. Imagine that, Pigeon Hollow, keeping up with the age of the internet! And, there were enough rooms at The Hideaway that if some of the crew doubled up, they could all stay there together during taping.

24

Happily making further plans for the crew as she stepped out of the shower, she began to rifle through her suitcase. Were two hundred dollar rhinestone-studded designer jeans too much for the honky tonk next door? They had to be more appropriate than one of her suits and that was what her choices amounted to at the moment. She pulled out a tank top and heels and she was good to go. Unfortunately, it was still two hours too early, so she booted up the laptop and checked her emails instead. She told herself she was anxious to get to the bar and start working on Jared. It definitely wasn't that she was excited to see him personally.

It is totally true that a watched pot never boils, or whatever that saying was, because the numbers on the digital read-out on the clock next to the bed changed more slowly than ever before. She made notes, returned phone calls, checked if she had enough blank consent forms for all the main characters in town and then finally it was just after eight. Perfect! Fashionably late. She did not want to arrive before Jared and his friend.

She checked her makeup, hiked up her boobs, and shoved cash and her room key into her pocket. Walking across the gravel drive to the bar, (all this damn gravel was killing her shoes) she anticipated that this bar would probably play a major role when it came time for taping. Drunks in a bar made for great television, too.

She heard the jukebox pumping out a lively country tune from outside the door. Once inside, she knew she was right about the bar being perfect for the show. It simply oozed small town atmosphere. Right down to the fact that the entire place quieted and every patron inside turned to look at her when she opened the door and stepped inside. Typical small town honky tonk.

Jared and looky, looky, the deputy, sat at a table just off the dance floor. Jared stood when she entered. Smiling, she made her way to them.

"Wow. You look great. And you actually own a pair of jeans." Jared glanced down at her approvingly.

"Of course. I'm not always dressed in stuffy business suits." He was looking pretty great himself. Although he was now wearing a shirt, and she'd liked the view that afternoon without it so much better.

He grinned at her. "Good to know. This here is my friend Bobby Barton. Bobby, this here's Mandy Morris."

She was sure that Jared had already filled his friend in about exactly who and what she was, but that was fine. She made no pretense about why she was in town.

Mandy extended her hand. "We've already met, sort of. Nice to see you again, deputy."

He shook her hand with a stern nod. "Bobby is fine. I'm off duty tonight, Ms. Morris."

Shaking her head she said, "Nuh, uh. It's Mandy. No business suits, no formal talk, tonight is for fun only."

Jared grinned wider, resting his hand lightly at the small of her back. "That is good to hear, too. What can I get you to drink?"

Supposing a good Cosmopolitan was out of the question here and a decent wine even more questionable, she settled on a light beer, which Jared procured for her lickity-split.

Finally, the three of them were all seated at a cozy little table so small her knee kept bumping into Jared's leg. He didn't move his leg out of the way, and neither did she. The occasional accidental, all right, maybe not so accidental, contact was nice. She hadn't bumped knees with a guy in awhile. She hadn't bumped anything else with a guy in a while either, come to think of it. She was long overdue for that.

Sipping on the longneck bottle— she had refused the glass so she'd blend in with the locals—Mandy remembered she'd forgotten to eat dinner. No wonder she was suddenly well on her way to getting tipsy.

She started small talk to take her mind of the heat radiating off of Jared's leg. "This is a great place. No wonder you come here."

Jared laughed. "It's also the only place, that's why we

26

come here."

Bobby didn't even smile. It seemed Bobby was going to be the tougher nut to crack, more so even than Jared. That was all right. She was up for a challenge. She was just getting her beer muscles.

"Well, I've been to more small towns and their bars in the last two weeks than I ever imagined I'd see in a lifetime. Having a basis for comparison, I can assure you, this is one of the better ones."

"Tell me where you've been, darlin'. What've you been doin' since I saw you last?" Jared relaxed back in his chair and stretched out one booted leg. She glanced at the long, lean, denim-clad leg and swallowed.

He wanted stories? She had stories. And what better way to take her mind off of how that leg would feel if she dared to put her hand on it?

Before she knew it, she was on her third beer (she'd bought the last round) and was still regaling them with stories of all the characters she'd met over the last few weeks of roaming the south in her rental car.

Still laughing from one of her tales, Jared excused himself to go to the men's room, leaving Mandy alone with Bobby, who wasn't laughing but at least wasn't looking hostile.

The deputy leaned forward when Jared was gone. "What are you still doin' in our town, Mandy?"

Leaning forward herself, she answered him. "Honestly? I'm still here hoping to convince this town that my offer to tape my show here is the best thing that ever happened to them. I've talked to a few of the business owners. Most of them were enthusiastic about the idea. Most, but not all. The Gordons still say no."

Bobby the deputy sipped his own beer and looked at her. "If you are so set on Pigeon Hollow, why not just do it and leave the Gordons out?"

She shook her head. "Without a signed consent form, I'll have to blur Jared out of any shots he gets his damn hunky, hot body into." Oh, shit. Had she said that out loud? Maybe Bobby didn't notice.

Bobby choked on his next swallow of beer. He'd noticed.

She stumbled on, trying to cover her embarrassment. "What Jared doesn't get, Bobby, is what I can do for this town. I stopped by today to get my nails done at—what's the name—Delilah's Salon."

"Delia's," Bobby corrected.

She threw a hand carelessly in the air. She was feeling looser than she had in a year. "Yeah, that's it. It was dead. I was the only person in there. Now, I bring in a crew of over a dozen here for two months. Think what an economic boost that will give to the small businesses in this town. Every one of those crew is going to need food, drink, lodging, salon services, gasoline, supplies..."

Shaking her head, Mandy took another slug of her light beer, which wasn't feeling so light as it went right to her head. She continued lecturing Bobby anyway. "Then, after the show hits, travelers who usually just whiz past on the expressway may decide to stop in the quaint little town they saw on television for a rest and a bite before continuing on. Maybe a bed and breakfast or two will open up and then the visitors will stay for the weekend. Don't the people of Pigeon Hollow deserve that chance? And who the hell is Jared Gordon to take it away from them?"

She stopped ranting when she noticed Bobby looking just above her shoulder. With a sinking feeling she knew what he was staring at, she turned slowly in her chair. "Jared. How long have you been standing there?"

"Long enough." There was an angry set to his jaw. His hazel eyes went from looking directly at her to a point somewhere up in the corner of the ceiling. It wasn't a good sign that he wouldn't even look at her.

Standing, she shook her head. "I didn't say anything just now that I wouldn't have said to your face, Jared. And you know every damn word of it is true. *That* is what's bothering you."

Nodding to Bobby, she slammed her beer bottle down on the table, spared one last glance at Jared, and then was out the door.

Chapter 5

Jared sat again and grabbed his beer, refusing to even look as the bar door swung shut behind Mandy.

"She's hot for you."

He looked at Bobby. "Are you fucking crazy? She's only here to get her damn show made."

Bobby shook his head. "Nope. Well, yeah. She wants this show made, but she could pick another town if she really wanted to. You heard the stories she told us. There's a ton of places more interestin' than Pigeon Hollow. I think she's so attached to this town because of you."

"No, you're wrong. She is single-minded and conniving and the only reason she sashayed her butt in here in those tight jeans tonight is so I'd agree to her show."

"She never kept it a secret she wants this show done here, and she didn't say anythin' that bad about you to me just now. I don't know why you're so pissed," Bobby pointed out.

He couldn't tell Bobby he was pissed off because he'd actually started to believe she was here because she was interested in him. But it was all about the damn show for her. Always had been, always would be. The more he thought about it, the angrier he got.

Jared slammed his beer bottle down onto the table and stood. "I'm goin' over there and givin' her a piece of my mind."

Bobby raised a brow. "You really want to do that?"

"Damn right I do. Why?"

Bobby shrugged. "Just making sure. You got a condom in your pocket?"

More than one, actually. That had been wishful thinking on his part. "Yeah. But what the hell does that have to do with anythin'?"

Bobby shook his head and shrugged, smiling.

Jared frowned deeply at his friend's strange behavior. "Watch my beer. I'll be right back."

Bobby laughed. "Yeah, OK." Was that sarcasm? He'd have to deal with Bobby later. Right now, he had other fish to fry.

Jared held on tightly to his anger until he'd made it across the parking lot. He found her rental car parked in front of the end unit. It was the only room with the lights on. It was probably the only room with an occupant.

Confident he had the right door, he knocked loudly before he had a chance to think and changed his mind. But when she opened the door wearing nothing but a short slip of silk, he stopped thinking all together.

He supposed he stepped into the room, although he didn't really remember doing so. But somehow, the door was closed behind him, and Mandy was standing so close, she was practically pressed against him.

Grasping for the reason he was here, he said, "You pissed me off tonight, darlin'."

"You've pissed me off every day since I met you, Jared Gordon."

Her blue eyes blazed into his and she didn't back down, or back up, even an inch. He swallowed hard and couldn't wrestle his eyes up from her hardened nipples protruding through the painfully thin silk. "Put something on so I can yell at you."

She snorted out a laugh. "No. You can just yell at me in what I'm wearing."

"Damn it! Why are you so stubborn?"

"Ha! You should talk."

He breathed in deep. "I am so angry at you I can't think straight, but I still want to fuck you until you can't walk. Why is that making me even angrier?" His hands fisted at his sides.

She crossed her arms across her chest in defiance. "I don't know. Maybe because you're too damn stubborn to give in to me on any little thing, you chauvinistic, backwoods…"

She didn't finish her sentence because his mouth was

suddenly covering hers. Her small fist hit him once in the chest and then grabbed his hair to pull his head closer to hers. He lifted her up. She wrapped her legs around his waist and her arms around his neck. He carried her like that across the room, misjudged the distance and smashed them both into the wooden dresser. She didn't complain. Neither did he.

With her perched on the edge of the dresser, he ground his pelvis into her. Pushing her short nightgown up to her hips, he discovered she wore no underwear underneath. They were both breathing fast; anger and sex will do that to you. He pulled back long enough to reinforce that fact to her. "I'm still mad at you."

She glared back, her hands still gripping his t-shirt tightly. "Good, because I'm still mad at you."

He bent his head again and shoved his tongue roughly into her mouth. She met him with her own, and matched thrust for thrust while pulling his shirt out of the waistband of his jeans.

He leaned back again and pulled the shirt over his head himself, flinging it to the floor. "I'm warnin' you. I'm too angry to be gentle."

She undid the button on his jeans and lowered the zipper. She freed his erection from his briefs with hands that were none too gentle while saying with short, clipped words, "Fine. I'm too drunk to care."

"Fine!" he shot back. He pulled a condom out of his pocket and covered himself. Grabbing her hips, he slid her forward and plunged into her warm wetness.

He was rough, pounding into her. She was rougher, drawing her nails down his back, and, he was sure, leaving scratches. She bit his shoulder. He marked her neck with his mouth in retaliation.

He didn't know how long it lasted. It could have been just a few minutes, it could have been half an hour. But finally, he felt himself teetering on the edge and exploded within her. Eyes squeezed shut, he pushed deep into her and enjoyed the final pulses of one very satisfying, albeit angry, release.

Mandy's hands grabbed his hips and held him close within her. Her breath started to come in small gasps and he felt her start to convulse around him. He held her tighter as she came, trembling in his arms, and all of his anger dissolved right then and there.

Jared closed his eyes and felt every pulse of her muscles. He kissed her hair and held her until the shuddering stopped. Sue Ann had been a real screamer. He'd liked it in the beginning, but it got old quick. And now, after this with Mandy, he had to wonder how much, if any of it, had been real with Sue Ann.

It was just one little orgasm. But it felt so right, so real, so natural to be sharing it with Mandy, to be in her and feel it right along with her. His feeling of satisfaction turned into a yearning to have her again…and again.

He suddenly very badly wanted to be in the nice comfy bed with her. "Hold on to me," he whispered against her hair, although it was probably unnecessary. Her arms and legs were still clasped around him, and she showed no signs of letting go. He lifted her and walked them both to the bed.

A bit of maneuvering and the use of a lot of leg muscles and he had lowered her gently to the bed, where she finally released her hold. That was a bit disappointing. He liked the feeling of her clinging to him. Pulling the horrid polyester motel comforter down, he covered her with the sheet and blanket. Since she had the AC on high, it was cold in the room, and she was starting to get goose bumps.

Mandy snuggled lower under the covers and Jared went into the bathroom to clean up. By the time he returned, she was sound asleep. He smiled. She looked so young and innocent sleeping, no longer the impatient, toe-tapping, finger-drumming, tough-as-nails businesswoman.

He slid down into the room's only chair and considered the situation. Bobby had known this was going to happen. Hence the strange condom discussion right before he left the bar. So why the hell hadn't Jared known? He supposed he was too angry and yes, too stubborn, to see what was right in front of him.

He wiggled his behind a bit in the chair, wondering why he was so uncomfortable, when he realized he was sitting on a folder of some sort. He pulled it out from underneath his butt and glanced at it. *Pigeon Hollow* was written in ladylike script across the front.

Feeling a bit guilty, he opened it anyway. Hand-written notes covered a page of lined legal paper. From what he could decipher, she'd taken notes on every one in town she'd found interesting, and what she'd written about him, made his eyes open wider. Things like 'cutie who gave directions at diner, investigate further'. And 'shoot Jared Gordon shirtless as often as possible--hottie!!!' Even his mother had made the cut. She was referred to as a 'Likeable version of Martha Stewart'. Mac, Delia, even Bobby, referred to only as 'The Deputy', were all listed here. And then there was another list. Provisions for the crew, plans on where they would stay, schedules for taping, possible locations.

Jared's eyes were opened to a number of facts. She was and had always been interested in him for this project. But judging by her descriptions of him, she'd been attracted to him personally, too, right from day one. And the other eye-opener was that this project, show, whatever it was, might actually be good for this town. Mandy was right. The people of Pigeon Hollow deserved this chance. Delia and Mac sure could use the extra business, and who was he to stop them?

In the back of the folder, he found a stack of blank consent forms. He considered barely a heartbeat before taking one copy out. He located a pen, also on the seat under his butt, and started to fill it out. He signed his name at the bottom, and placed it in the middle of the desk on top of the folder.

He glanced at the still sleeping Mandy, grabbed his shirt off the floor and slipped quietly out of the door, making sure it was locked behind him. In the bar parking lot, he got into his truck. He didn't feel like talking to Bobby again just yet. Instead, he started the engine and headed for the farm. As he drove, he hoped he'd done the right thing. And then, thinking how by just signing the paper he'd insured Mandy would be around for two more months, he hoped even more that he'd done it for the right reasons.

Chapter 6

Mandy woke up with what felt like cotton balls in her mouth. She flung her arm over her face to block out the dim light filtering through the curtains. Why did she feel like such crap? As her body and mind began to wake, she felt the pull of sore muscles in her legs, and in other places too, muscles that hadn't been used in a very long time.

Holy cow! She sat straight up in bed. Bad idea, she realized, as she got lightheaded and felt the stabbing pain behind her eyes. She didn't know what was worse, her hangover, or the fact that she'd had sex with Jared Gordon. Shit! She couldn't believe she'd broken her own rule and mixed business with pleasure. Very, very nice pleasure, but pleasure none the less. She'd only intended on flirting, not actually having sex with him.

She made a vow to never drink on an empty stomach again. As she stumbled to the bathroom to take care of her near to exploding bladder, she noted with interest that she wasn't vowing to herself to never have sex with Jared again. If her fuzzy brain remembered accurately, it had been incredible.

But on second thought, of course it was great. After all, he was one unbelievably attractive specimen. But often, in her experience, the reality didn't live up to the exterior packaging. No false advertising here; in Jared's case, what you see is what you get.

She had to stop thinking of him like this. She had done a bad, bad thing. In a business where far too many women used sex to make their way to the top, she had vowed never to do so. And she had paid the penalty, too, on more than one occasion, and been passed over for a less qualified bimbo who wasn't opposed to sweating up the casting couch with an executive.

Now that she was finally in a good place in her career, she still couldn't afford to compromise her morals. But she needn't worry, last night with Jared would be just that. One night. That wasn't any sort of vow, just the cold hard reality of the situation. She'd pissed him off at the bar and he still hated the idea of the show. In fact, he'd reminded her enough times how angry he was at her all throughout the incredible sex.

Sighing, she realized she would just have to get over losing Pigeon Hollow and use her second choice. Somehow, she'd make it work, she always did. Although, she had a feeling giving up Pigeon Hollow would be easier than giving up Jared Gordon.

Face washed and teeth brushed, she pulled her hair into a quick bun and shuffled over to her suitcase. She would get dressed, get something to eat at the diner, and drive to the airport without looking back. She felt a tugging in her belly and wrote it off to her hangover. It definitely was *not* disappointment that she would never see Jared again.

She walked past the desk on her way to the suitcase, stopped, walked backwards and stood there, just staring down at the single piece of paper. Her face grew hot, her heart began to pound, her hands trembled. If she had been a cartoon character, the top of her head would have blown off by now. She reached out one shaky hand and picked up the signed consent form.

That one piece of paper, with that one signature, *Jared Gordon*, turned her into exactly the kind of woman she'd spent her entire career trying to avoid being. Jared had signed the paper after she'd had sex with him. He might as well have just left cash on the nightstand.

~

Still in a post-coital daze, Jared instinctively worked his way through the morning chores. Good thing his body remembered what to do, because his mind was back at The Hideaway with Mandy. It was still early, he liked to get the heavy chores done before the heat of the day struck, but she might be waking up about now.

Knowing her, his little bundle of contained energy, she couldn't lounge around long. He imagined her in bed still wearing the little silk thing she'd been in when he'd left her. Why had he left her? It would have been really nice to wake up with her in his arms. He laughed to himself. He knew why he'd left her. She was probably going to be pissed as hell when she woke up and remembered what they'd done.

Jared had a feeling Mandy wouldn't like that she'd given in to her desires, especially since she'd claimed to be drunk last night. That was hard to believe, he'd had as much to drink as her and he'd felt fine. Although, she was a tiny thing, and three beers could do it to someone who wasn't used to drinking.

Yup, she was really going to be pissed all right. Mmm, mmm! He liked her even more when she was angry. Although, maybe when she saw the signed form, she'd be happy. Then she'd be grateful. He definitely could handle her showing him her gratitude.

He hopped up into the seat of the tractor thinking how, angry or grateful, he couldn't wait until he saw her again. Whistling the whole drive out to the manure pile, where he dumped the contents of the tractor's bucket, he turned and was on the trip back to the barn when he spotted her car.

Hot damn, she was earlier than he'd hoped. He raised the throttle and flew across the field so fast, he was nearly bounced out of the seat when he hit a bump. When he was close enough, he abandoned the tractor and met her in front of the barn.

Mandy's eyes were narrowed and she was huffing and puffing and looking so angry, he had to smile. She slapped a paper against his chest. Grabbing it before it fluttered to the ground, he saw it was the consent form he'd signed the night before.

"Did you sign that form just because I had sex with you?" she spat at him in a fury.

He raised a brow and decided to tease her further. "No. Did you sleep with me just so I'd sign the form?"

"No! You arrogant bastard! What the hell do you think I am?" She was working her way into quite a rant.

Lord, she was so hot when she was angry. Jared couldn't contain his attraction for his little hellcat any longer. Grabbing her with both hands, he crushed his lips to hers.

She mumbled against his mouth for a second, still trying to yell at him, until she gave herself to the kiss. Leaning into him, the only sound was her soft groan. With her arms around his neck, her body pressed against his, Jared was tempted to take her right there up against the tractor.

Mandy pulled away. "Do you really think that I slept with you so you'd sign?"

He shook his head. "No. I never even considered that thought."

Mandy looked up at him with a frown. "Then why did you sign?"

"I realized you were right. This town could use the business, and who the hell am I to stop them? And how could I not sign after I read your notes calling me a 'cutie' and a 'hottie'." He wiggled his eyebrows at her and had to deflect her hands as she slapped at his chest.

"You read my notes? Ooo, you are so infuriating!"

He laughed and captured her hands in his. "And you are irresistible when you're mad, and I plan on getting you angry as often as I can."

He leaned in and kissed her again, softly on the lips.

She pulled her head back and shook her head. "You really know how to push my buttons, Jared Gordon."

Jared growled low in his throat. "I'd like a chance to get to push your buttons again, real soon."

Her chest rose and fell beneath the silky top as she breathed in deeply. She shook her head. "This is impossible. I shouldn't be involved with you at all. But definitely not once the taping starts."

He considered that. "Fine, if it's a choice between being with you or taping this show, the decision is easy." He grasped the consent form with two hands and was about to rip it in half when she stopped him.

"Wait!"

He paused.

She sighed and gave in. "We'll figure something out."

He wanted clarification before he released his hold on her precious consent form. "What exactly does that mean?"

She sighed so deeply it was like the weight of the world was on her shoulders. "It means that we have to be very discreet, and we may have to sneak around after hours, but we can probably swing some time together once the crew is here."

He broke out into a delighted grin. Sneaking around sounded like fun. He hadn't 'snuck' since he was a teen. He nodded and handed the paper back to her. "OK then. But I'm gonna hold you to that."

She folded it neatly in thirds and slipped it into an invisible pocket in her skirt. She hung her head. "I have no doubt that you will."

He lifted her chin. "You want me as much as I want you, darlin'. Admit that to me, just once."

"This is hard for me, Jared."

He resisted making a joke about how 'hard' it was for him, too, and was extremely proud of his own restraint. Instead, he said something that he hoped was actually helpful. "It's only hard for you because you are always 'work, work, work'. You need to take time to slow down, smell the roses, kiss the farmer..." He smiled and lowered his mouth to just a breath from hers. His hand slid up her thigh and under her short skirt. "Let me show you how relaxed I can make you."

His finger slid beneath the elastic of her underwear and she drew in a quick breath. "Jared. We're in public."

He'd never thought of his farm as public before. "We're fine. Don't worry."

She swallowed hard and her eyes drifted shut as he found her sweet spot. "Your mother."

"Out shoppin' two towns away. She'll be gone for hours." He nibbled on her earlobe.

"Your employees." She was sounding breathless.

"Out fixin' a fence on the far side of the property. Won't see them 'til lunch." He ran a tongue down her throat and felt the pulse hammering away. He noticed the small bruise he'd left there the night before and smiled. Yup, she was his now, for all to see.

She took a shaky breath and started to tremble. It appeared she had nothing else to say. He nuzzled her neck. "What's the matter, darlin'. Run out of problems? You may have to actually enjoy yourself."

She was panting softly, but still managed to start to bitch at him. "You are so…oh…" She never got to finish.

One hand still very busy, he wrapped his free arm around her waist as he felt her knees start to fold. "Hold on to me, darlin'. I got you."

Mandy clung to his neck as she came. He didn't let up until she was slumped against him. It was almost as good feeling and hearing her orgasm as having one of his own. Almost, but not quite, and it left Jared with a hard-on that he could hammer nails with.

Coming back to her senses, even though he wished she wouldn't, Mandy pulled the bottom of her skirt down until she was decent again and looked up at him with heavily lidded baby blues. "I have to leave for LA for a bit to get everything ready for the taping. But when I get back, this," she indicated their current situation with one finger, "is one of the things we can not do once the camera crews are here."

He laughed, but was perfectly serious when he hinted, "So I guess a blow job is out of the question then?"

She actually blushed. "Out here in the open? Yes. Definitely out of the question."

He raised a brow. "How about in the hay room?"

Her eyes opened wide and before she could protest, he grabbed her hand and pulled her into the barn.

Jared sat on a waist-high stack of hay bales and pulled her between his legs. She looked around the room lit only by the sunlight filtering through the cracks in the walls. "I've never 'rolled in the hay' before."

He laughed. "I don't recommend it. It's itchy. This was my brother Jimmy's favorite hiding spot when he had a girl, not mine. But it'll serve our purposes."

Her eyes opened wide. "You have a brother?"

"Yup. You didn't know? I've got two."

He could see the wheels in her head turning, still thinking about work, even now. "Do they live around here? Do they look anything like you?"

He'd consider that last question a compliment but Jared still couldn't tell her his brothers were both covert special operatives and couldn't be on her little show.

He'd just have to get her mind back on him and off them and work. "Hey there now, darlin'. They're both taken, and I plan on being more Gordon than you can handle as it is." He placed her one hand on the bulge in the crotch of his jeans. "Forget about them and leave me somethin' to remember you by while you're away in LA."

She raised her brow. "Oh, believe me. You're not going to forget me anytime time soon." With his help, she made quick work of the belt and fly on his jeans.

Booted feet still on the floor, he leaned back against the bales until he was staring at the cobweb-filled ceiling. Maybe one day, they would actually make it to a bed, he thought. And that was the last coherent thought he had once she pushed his briefs aside and took him in her mouth.

She felt so good, he grit his teeth and prolonged it for what he considered an impressively long time. He was making all the appropriate comments to let her know how much he appreciated what she was doing but she still finally raised her head and accused him, "Are you holding back?"

He lifted his head and grinned at her. "Yup."

She frowned. "Well, stop it! This is a lot of work."

That's why it's called a job! He laughed at his silent little joke but didn't say it out loud to her, figuring he was in too delicate of a position to piss her off. "Anything you say, darlin'."

He stroked her hair and lowered his own head onto the

hay again, settling in for a lot more enjoyment, until Mandy did something that made him shoot off like a cannon.

He sat up like a shot himself. "Jeez, woman! You can't go stickin' your fingers in a man's private place like that."

She laughed. "Serves you right for holding back. Besides, it worked, didn't it?"

He grabbed her and pulled until she was sitting across his lap. "Just remember that what's good for the goose, is good for the gander."

"And that means what?"

He cupped her ass in one hand. "It means you better keep an eye on that sweet ass of yours, darlin', because I sure will be."

"I'll try and remember that." She pulled away. "But now, I have to go."

He drew her back and nuzzled her breasts through her blouse. "No, you don't."

She laughed. "Yes, I do. First of all, this suit probably cost as much as one of your horses and it shouldn't be doing any more rolling in the hay. And second, I have to catch my flight back to LA."

He sighed and released her, sliding her gently back onto her feet on the hay strewn floor. "First of all, there is no way that suit cost anything near one of my horses, darlin'. But I'll forgive that insult, bein' you're a city girl. Second, go catch your flight, because the sooner you get to LA and do what you gotta do, the sooner you'll be back here with me."

He kissed her softly and then watched her shake her head in the dim light. "God, this is such a bad idea."

Standing and holding both of her hands tightly in his, he stepped forward until he was pressed against her. "Do I have to prove to you again that it's not, darlin'?"

She stepped back. "No. You don't. And I don't have time now, anyway. This is a problem I have to deal with on my own."

He frowned. He hadn't thought of her being with him as a problem, but she seemed to see it as one. "A problem

shared by two is only half as big, darlin'. Remember that."
He lowered his head and kissed her long and hard as she let
his tongue tangle with hers. Then he pulled away. "That was
something to remember me by."

"Don't worry. I won't be forgetting you anytime soon,
either, Jared Gordon." She turned and left. And he realized
he was standing alone in the hay room with his jeans
hanging wide open.

He righted himself, and it was a damn good thing he did,
because he heard footsteps in the barn, followed by Bobby's
voice.

"Well, well, well. You two havin' a little romp in the
hay room?"

Jared rolled his eyes and slowly shook his head. Good
thing Bobby hadn't been a few minutes earlier. Although,
being deputy sheriff, Bobby had probably caught every
young person in this town doing it at least once.

"Don't bother tryin' to deny it. I saw your city girl
gettin' into her car. There was hay in her hair. She looked
like she wanted to crawl into a hole in the ground when I
pointed it out to her. Never thought I'd see that one blush,
but she was blushin' all right."

"I'm not denyin' it." Jared blew out a breath. Poor
Mandy. She was having enough trouble as it was with this
situation, although why, he didn't know. But here his
supposed friend was teasing her. "And don't give her a hard
time anymore, Bobby. I like her. A lot."

Bobby laughed. "What else is new?"

He shook his head. "Nah. I mean it."

"This isn't just 'two adults scratchin' an itch' the way it
was with Sue Ann?"

Jared shook his head violently. "No way. This is nothin'
like Sue Ann and me." He blew out a frustrated breath.
"Damn, I've got it bad. I miss Mandy already and she's
barely out of the drive. What the hell am I gonna do when
the show is over and she goes back to California for good?"

"Show?" Yup, Bobby was about as surprised as Jared

thought he'd be at that news.

He nodded. "I signed her consent form to be in the show."

Bobby raised a brow. "Really? Hmm."

"Hmm, what?" Jared accused.

"I'm just wonderin' why, that's all."

"Because it's good for this town, that's why." Jared didn't add that it was good for him, too.

He figured he had two months to convince Mandy she couldn't live without him. That should be plenty of time. Hell, he was a Gordon, after all.

Chapter 7

Mandy had never, in her entire career, mixed business with pleasure. Yet here she was driving as fast as she could from the airport, rushing back to Jared Gordon. And she was actually feeling not so bad about it.

She couldn't deny the attraction between them was there from the very beginning, regardless of their business dealings. And she believed him when he said he hadn't signed the consent form because she'd slept with him, but because it was good for the town.

She'd finally stopped beating herself up about all that had happened between them after the first week back in LA. After that, she started to enjoy the idea of being Jared's 'city girl', as he called her. How crazy was that? A horseman from Pigeon Hollow and a television producer from LA, they were taking the term 'long distance relationship' to a whole new level.

Of course, Jared's nightly phone calls helped bridge that long distance. His smooth southern voice could, and did, do things to her that most men couldn't accomplish with their entire body. Not to say that she wasn't looking forward to enjoying his whole body, too. She definitely was.

The rest of the production crew had flown with her, and were currently divided among a few rented minivans, along with their equipment. They'd go directly to The Hideaway to get settled in, but Mandy had claimed she had errands to run so she could be alone in the car and go directly to Jared.

She slowed on Main Street and smiled. It was nice to know some things didn't change. In front of the diner was a Gordon Equine truck parked next to what must be Bobby's official deputy sheriff's car. It looked like she wasn't going to have to drive all the way to the farm after all.

It was lunchtime, so there was an uncharacteristic amount of traffic and no parking spaces in front of the diner. Mandy was forced to drive further until she finally found a spot. She turned off the engine, got out and locked the door behind her, but it was an effort to restrain herself from simply abandoning the car and sprinting to the diner.

As it was, she was so focused on the single-minded goal of reaching Jared that she wasn't paying attention to where she was walking. As if out of nowhere, the chubby, ponytail-wearing waitress from the diner and a trashily dressed woman with a bad bleach job smacked directly into her. Mandy stumbled, but it wasn't the physical blow, it was what they told her, that nearly brought her to her knees.

~

Jared finished the last bite of his hamburger and glanced over at the counter. As tempting as the pies in the diner's glass display case looked, he knew Mama had baked a fresh blackberry pie that morning. That was worth waiting for, no question. Besides that, he was sitting in the glare of the sun and it was hot, AC or not. The diner was more crowded than usual so he and Bobby had been forced to take the only table available, even though it was up against the front window.

But the real reason he was in a hurry to get out of there, the only reason that mattered, was that Mandy was flying in today. She said she would drive out to the farm as soon as she could after settling the crew in town. His heart raced at the thought of seeing her again. Phone sex with her was great, but it was not the real thing.

He threw cash for his meal on the table and was about to tell Bobby he was out of there when he noticed Bobby lean forward, looking out the window.

"Is Mandy coming back today?"

Jared nearly jumped from his seat. "Yeah, is she outside?"

Bobby let out a breath. "Yeah, with Sue Ann."

"Oh, shit." Jared launched himself away from the table, sending the chair flying behind him. He was out the door and on the sidewalk for what seemed like forever before Bobby caught up with him.

He strode forward to the group of three women: Mandy, Sue Ann, and Misty. The look on Mandy's face didn't bode well.

He reached out to touch her. "Mandy, darlin'."

She looked down at his hand, slowly shook her head, and backed away from him.

Jared took a step forward and grabbed her by both shoulders. He watched her close her eyes. "Let go of me, Jared."

"No. I don't know what Sue Ann told you, but you have to give me a chance to defend myself." Shit, that had sounded like he was guilty of something. God only knew what the hell Sue Ann had told her.

Mandy was breathing hard enough to hyperventilate. "Bobby, make him take his hands off of me *now*."

Bobby was beside him suddenly. "Jared."

Jared shook his head. "No."

He felt Bobby's hand on his shoulder. A gentle warning, he supposed. Wasn't this laughable? His best friend protecting his own girlfriend from him! As if he could ever hurt Mandy. He shook his head at the ridiculous idea and dropped his hands from her shoulders. With one last hurt-filled look, Mandy turned and got into her car, peeling out into traffic as she drove away.

Jared turned on Sue Ann. "What the hell did you tell her?"

Sue Ann shrugged. "Nothin' but the truth."

Jared stepped closer and glared down at the girl he used to actually think was attractive. "And what warped version of the *truth* was that?"

"I'm late."

Jared's stomach clenched and his lunch threatened to work its way back up his throat. "No. That's impossible. You know we used birth control every time."

She shrugged. "Birth control fails."

"You said you were on the pill *and* I used a condom every single fucking time! Don't you dare lie and tell me you're pregnant by me." Then a thought struck him, clear as day. "Who else have you been screwin', Sue Ann?"

48

She blanched, and he was sure he'd hit on the truth. But she still denied it.

"Fine. We'll go to the doc for a paternity test today. Right fucking now, Sue Ann." He grabbed her arm roughly, and Bobby was beside him again. "Back off, Bobby. Leave me and the supposed mother of my child alone until I can get the doc to prove she's a liar."

Sue Ann dug her heels into the sidewalk. "No, we can't go to the doc. I mean, I'm sure those tests can hurt the baby. I refuse to have one."

Just then, Misty piped in. "Sue Ann, hadn't you better take the pregnancy test you just bought first? You're only like a day late."

Jared's eyes opened wide and he squeezed her arm harder. "What?"

"Jared. Enough." Bobby's hand covered his. He released her and watched his handprint on her arm turn from white to red.

"You don't even know if you're pregnant and you're telling my girlfriend about it." He shook his head at her. "I'm embarrassed I even let you get me angry, Sue Ann, because you are nothin' but pitiful. God help the man that ends up with you."

He spun on his heel and strode to his truck, fumbling in his jeans pocket for the keys.

Once again, Bobby was beside him. "Where you goin', Jared?"

"To The Hideaway. I hope to hell she went there and not the airport."

"I'll drive. Give me your keys."

"The hell you will."

"Jared, give me the damn keys. You're so angry, you're shakin'. Neither you nor Mandy should be drivin' right now. Since I can't do anythin' about her, I'm doin' somethin' about you."

Jared huffed out a breath and slapped the keys in Bobby's outstretched hands. "Fine. But hurry up."

Bobby scowled. "I'm a deputy sheriff. I can't go speeding down Main Street, even if I am in your truck."

Jared shook his head. "I knew I should have drove."

The trip to the motel seemed to take forever, although Jared knew it was only a few miles. When they finally arrived, he saw the place was packed with vans and people unloading them. The crew for the show. Jared took their presence as a good sign. No matter how hurt she was, Mandy was in charge of the production of this show. She wouldn't leave town, if only because of that.

His anger at Sue Ann blossomed all over again as he knocked on the door of the unit where Mandy's car was parked. A cute young thing opened the door a crack. "Yes?"

For the first time, he wondered if he had the wrong door. "Is Mandy Morris in this room?"

"Who are you?"

Jared's instincts told him Mandy was hiding inside. He pushed his palm against the door, only to find the chain was engaged. He leaned into the crack. "Mandy. Please, darlin'. Talk to me."

With Bobby standing directly behind him, he knew he couldn't break the door in to get to Mandy, as tempting as it was. The girl guarding the door looked at someone inside the room, then turned back to him. "Excuse us for a minute." Then the door slammed in his face.

Jared ran his hands over his face with frustration, and felt Bobby's hand on his shoulder. Jared set his jaw. "Bobby, if you say 'I told you so' about Sue Ann one more time, I'll clock you. Deputy or not."

Bobby stepped around him. "Well, I'd like to see you try. But what I was going to say was, she'll listen, eventually. It just might take a bit of time. But don't you go doin' anything crazy in the meantime."

Jared listened, and although he didn't like what he heard, Bobby was right. He had to keep his cool here. Mandy was strung so tight; he always knew that if she ever snapped, it would be really bad. He'd assumed her work would be the

50

thing to eventually throw her over the edge, but it seemed Sue Ann had gotten to her first.

The door opened fully and the girl walked out, eyeing him the entire time. Jared didn't wait for an invitation and shot inside. One look at Mandy confirmed his suspicion. She'd cracked, and it was bad.

She sat in the room's only chair. Head buried in her arms while she hugged her knees, he couldn't see her face, but he heard her sniffle as she rocked herself.

His heart broke. He bent and scooped her up in his arms, sitting in the chair with her in his lap. He kissed her hair and gently rocked her. "Shhh, darlin', don't cry."

Her soft sniffles turned into all out heaving, gasping sobs. She always did tend to be contrary, and now was no different. He shook his head, held her tighter, and let her cry until she was all cried out. Since she was never one to do anything halfway, that took a while.

He knew she was finished when she raised her head and one tiny fist smashed into his arm. "You bastard!" He nearly smiled. He'd take anger over tears any day. Luckily, he'd stopped himself from actually smiling at her, because that would have probably earned him more than just a punch in the arm at that moment.

"Darlin'. I'm going to tell you the god's honest truth, and if you don't want to believe me, Bobby is right outside and he'll back me up. I admit to being a stupid idiot who used to sleep with Sue Ann, but I ended it before you ever came to this town and turned my life upside down." At her frown, he added, "I meant that last part in a good way."

"But she said…"

"She lied. I'll do anything you want to prove it. I won't let her or anythin' else take you away from me, darlin'."

Her face crumpled, but she threw her arms around his neck and held on tight, so he figured it was a good thing, until she pulled back and looked fiercely at him. "But Jared, really. Her? Her roots are so far past a touch up, her hair is practically two-tone, she's wearing blue eye shadow and a tube top! How in the world could the same man be attracted to both her and me? We might as well be from different planets."

He snorted. "You're telling me!"

She held her hands out in an 'I'm waiting for an answer' gesture.

He gave in. "All right. I'm gonna tell you somethin' about men. There are women we're attracted to for a night or two because they're easy. And then there are other women we are attracted to for the long haul, because they're keepers."

She considered that for a moment. "Which one am I?"

Jared laughed out loud. "Darlin'. There ain't nothin' easy about you! You're the hardest damn woman I've ever had the pleasure of knowing." Yup, he thought, she was a keeper. And somehow, someway, he'd find a way to keep her here in Pigeon Hollow with him. Jared snuggled his face against Mandy's hair. "We all right?"

He felt her nod. Running his hand up and down her spine, he kissed each closed eye-lid softly. "Can I show you how much I've missed you now?'

She opened her still tear-reddened eyes and looked up at him. She took a shaky breath. "Yeah, I think I'd like that."

He smiled and kissed her lips. Then closed his own eyes and groaned. "Bobby drove my truck. He's outside with no ride back to his car in town."

"Christy can take him."

"Whose Christy?"

"My associate producer. The one who convinced me to let you in the door when I didn't want to."

"Well then, I owe her already for that. I might as well owe her for driving Bobby back to town, too." Jared paused. "You really weren't goin' to let me in?"

She pursed her lips. "I guess I would have given in eventually. Either that, or you would have broken down the door."

He laughed. "You think you know me pretty well, don't

ya?"

"Mmm, hmm." She nodded.

"Then tell me what I'm thinking right now."

She smiled. "I'm sitting in your lap. I can feel exactly what you're thinking about right now."

He had been going to tell her he loved her. But he decided to save that for some moonlit romantic night in the near future.

Instead, he picked her up and carried her to the bed. "Can't hide anything from you, darlin'."

"No, you can't. You better remember that."

He smiled. "I surely will, darlin'. I surely will."

The End

THE BALLPLAYER

Chapter 1
Ten Years Ago

Lizzie Barton sat on the hard wooden bench and watched the batter swing and miss. The pitch had been much too high and inside. If he had only let it go without swinging, it would have been called a ball instead of a strike. But Jared Gordon was never one to give in on anything, even a bad pitch. She shook her head and smiled to herself.

Cute, stubborn and a definite heartbreaker—that described all three Gordon brothers, Jared, Jack and Jimmy.

Lizzie's sister, Mary Sue, had spent a few steamy nights with Jack Gordon once upon a time. That was before Jack followed Jimmy into the service. Mary Sue had acted all hurt by that, but Jack had never made any pretense about sticking around Pigeon Hollow after graduation. Lizzie didn't blame him one bit for wanting to get away. As far as small towns went, this one was among the smallest.

Lizzie watched as Jared finally connected with a pitch and sent it flying into the outfield, right over the head of the center fielder. She clapped and cheered as the players on the loaded bases ran home. Jared rounded the bases and brought up the rear.

He was a cutie, all right. And unlike his brothers, he was sticking around Pigeon Hollow to help his mama run her breeding farm. Too bad Lizzie felt about as romantic toward Jared as she did about her older brother Bobby.

Nope. There wasn't a boy in her town who made her heart go pitter pat since Cole Ryan had left for college on a baseball scholarship. But that little crush was totally one-sided on her part. He was a friend of Bobby's, and steered clear of his friend's little sister out of respect. At least that's what she told herself. It was easier to think that than admit that he just wasn't attracted to her younger self, with her pigtails, mouthful of braces and baby fat.

But now, it was a whole new ballgame. College was out for the summer. Cole should be coming home soon. More importantly, today was Lizzie's eighteenth birthday. Yup. Now, she was a legal, brace-free adult. She was old enough to vote and she was old enough to do whatever she wanted with Cole Ryan. All she knew was, her brother Bobby better not get in the way, if he knew what was good for him!

Lizzie must have been frowning because her best friend Savannah Jordan sat down next to her and said, "What'd I miss? And why are you looking so angry about it?"

Lizzie smiled. "I'm not angry. And you just missed Jared hitting a grand slam."

"Darn. I love watching his cute little buns run around the bases. I knew I shouldn't have been late." Anna, what her friends called her for short, shook her head in disgust while obviously searching the field for Jared's butt. Unfortunately for her, he had already high-fived the entire team and was back sitting on the asset in question.

"Why are you so late? When I talked to you on the phone, you said you were on your way."

"Well, maybe you'll forgive me, Miss Punctuality, when I tell you why. I stopped to get gas on my way here and guess who was there?"

Lizzie's eyes opened wide. The Ryan family, as in Cole Ryan, owned the local gas station. She swallowed and tried not to let her friend see how excited she was. Better to keep her intentions for this summer secret just in case she was being delusional about the possibility of Cole being interested in her now that she looked more woman than child. "Hmm, let me guess. Cole?"

"Yup!" Anna cried with glee. "And he is looking hhhot!" She made the one syllable word into more like two or three.

"So you had to stop and talk to him, of course."

"Of course, what do you think? I'm not crazy. And you know what he told me?"

Lizzie couldn't imagine. But jealousy reared its ugly head at the thought of Cole telling Anna anything. "No, but I bet you're going to tell me."

Anna frowned. "Maybe I won't. What are you, PMSing or something?"

Lizzie just shook her head. "No. I'm just not in the mood for intrigue, so are you going to tell me or not? I don't care either way." This pretending she wasn't interested in Cole was harder than she thought it would be.

"He's dropping out of college!" Anna announced triumphantly.

"What? Is he crazy? He's on a full-ride scholarship for baseball to the best college in the state and he's dropping out? Why?"

Anna smiled, as if enjoying that she had information that Lizzie wanted. Why were they best friends again? "He got picked up by a minor league team. He's going to play pro-ball starting this summer! He only came home to see his parents before starting training."

"Jeez. Wow. I guess that's good. But still, he should get an education to fall back on just in case anything happens. You know athletes get injured or dumped by their teams all the time."

Anna, Miss Live-for-the-Moment, rolled her eyes. "Chances like this don't come along every day."

"Neither do full-ride scholarships," Lizzie countered.

"You just think that college is so important because you're a bookworm and got into your first choice with a academic scholarship."

Darn right! Lizzie had worked hard to make that happen. Studying every night instead of going out on dates, taking on a heavy course load of college prep classes her senior year instead of partying like everyone else.

Anna continued, undaunted. "The rest of us *normal* people don't think like that, but whatever. So, what do you want to do for your birthday tonight?"

Lizzie considered. The drive-in theater was about the only entertainment around Pigeon Hollow, besides the bowling alley. Although, given the choice between being the fifth wheel at the drive-in with Anna and her current boyfriend while they made out in the backseat or going bowling, she probably should choose bowling. But neither seemed good enough to celebrate her eighteenth birthday.

Anna jumped in. "You know what we can do? I heard there's a party by the river tonight. Some of the guys home from college got a beer keg and everything."

Lizzie frowned. She wasn't much of a beer drinker, but Cole might be there. "The sheriff always catches kids parked down by the river."

"I know. That's why I can't wait for your brother to officially become a deputy, so we'll be exempt."

Lizzie laughed. "Yeah, right! He'll only be twice as hard on me as he is on everyone else in town."

Anna considered that and nodded. "You're probably right. But anyway, the party is off in the woods so the sheriff won't find it."

Lizzie thought that was doubtful, but since it was a better idea than any of the other options, she agreed. "All right. What time you want to go?"

~

Cole drove his convertible and enjoyed the wind in his hair. The car was new to him, even though it was used. It was a gift from his father for getting picked up by a minor league team. Cole might be starting out in the minor leagues, but he could feel it in his gut, he'd be playing in the majors soon. Then, he'd be buying his parents brand-new cars as gifts. Maybe he could even talk his father into selling the service station and retiring.

The stars shown brightly in the dark sky as Cole edged closer to the river on his way to some keg party. The deal was that everyone attending this supposedly secret gathering that every kid in town seemed to know about was to park far away from the river. That was so the sheriff wouldn't find them. Cole hated to leave his new car like that, but he had no choice. He reluctantly parked on a dirt road beneath a tree, put up the roof, locked the car, and pocketed his keys. He heard sounds of a party from where he was parked and, following the noises, began to walk.

As he got closer, he realized he was actually looking forward to this party. He couldn't wait to tell some of the guys he'd graduated with the good news. Although, Pigeon Hollow was so small and everyone was so in everyone else's business, he was pretty sure there was no one left in town to tell. Even so, he would enjoy having a few beers and relaxing with some friends before he went off to start the adult life that awaited him.

He smelled the bonfire before he saw it. Thinking that starting a fire was not only risky, but also a good way to lead the sheriff right to them, he stumbled out of the trees and into a clearing. The moment the group of guys circling the keg saw him, a cheer rose. Smiling, he ambled over. A beer cup was thrust at him and the group took turns shaking his hand and congratulating him.

"Hey, Cole. You should have been at the game today. Jared here hit a grand slam! Maybe he'll be joining you in the majors one day," one of the guys informed him.

"Sounds good to me." Cole slapped Jared on the back. "I wouldn't mind another local boy there in the city with me."

Jared shook his head. "Nope, big city life's not for me. I'm stayin' right here. But is was nice to rub it into the other team's faces today that Pigeon Hollow doesn't lose to anybody!"

Another cheer rose, and Cole shook his head and laughed. He better drink his fill fast, because as noisy as these guys were, this secret party was on borrowed time already.

Cole glanced around and noticed that scattered amid the guys were a few girls milling around. And among them, tucked off in a corner looking embarrassed while holding a cup but not drinking, was Bobby Barton's little sister, Lizzie. Only she didn't look like she used to. Somehow since he'd been away for a year at school, she'd absolutely blossomed. Her dark hair was still long and wavy, but it wasn't in pigtails anymore. And she still wore t-shirts and denim miniskirts, but boy-oh-boy, did she fill them out.

If Bobby ever saw him lookin at Lizzie like this... Taking a closer look around the clearing, he realized that although Lizzie was there, Bobby wasn't.

"Hey, where's Bobby at?" he asked the closest person.

"He's been workin' days at the grocery store and takin' classes at night at the community college. Getting a degree in criminal justice or somethin' so he can join the sheriff's department."

Cole nearly choked on his beer. "Really? The sheriff's department, wow." He felt guilty he'd lost touch with his best friend from high school while away at college. It wasn't intentional; it was just tough playing ball in college while trying to keep up with classes.

He glanced at Lizzie again. She'd always had the trademark Barton dark hair and brilliant blue eyes that made all three of the siblings distinguishable in town. But now, Lizzie had the body of a woman, too. What a change from the little rugrat in pigtails who used to trail along behind him and Bobby for as long as he could remember.

He smiled at the memory and started to work his way over to her. Hell, it couldn't hurt to say hi and ask about Bobby.

He reached her side, and she nervously smiled up at him just as all hell broke loose. Spotlights suddenly appeared as the sheriff and two deputies strode into the clearing, yelling for everyone to stay right where they were. Cole didn't think twice. He flung his and Lizzie's beer cups into the bushes, grabbed her and pulled her into the shelter of the woods.

They ran through the trees, Cole leading Lizzie by the hand as he tried to avoid tripping over stumps and getting whipped in the face by branches. When they'd managed to get a good distance away from the clearing, he stopped and listened for anyone who might be pursuing them. But the only sound he heard was Lizzie breathing and his own heart pounding. "I don't think they saw us leave."

He barely saw her nod in the dim moonlight filtering

through the pines. "Thank you for getting me out of there. I can't tell you how much trouble I would have been in if my parents or even worse, Bobby, had to bail me out of jail. And on my eighteenth birthday, too."

He turned fully toward her and grabbed both her hands in his. "Today is your eighteenth birthday? Well, we can't have it ruined, now can we? Come on. My car is parked not far from here. We'll celebrate, just the two of us."

She smiled at him. "I'd like that." Then she hesitated. "But…"

"But what?" He squeezed her hands harder.

"I'm worried about Anna. She was at the party with me."

He raised a brow, surprised Anna and Lizzie were still friends. Two more different people you would never find. "Savannah Jordan? I wouldn't worry about her if I were you. She can definitely take care of herself. Besides, if we go back to look for her, chances are we'll get caught." And he seriously doubted Anna was worrying about where Lizzie was. She was probably off sucking face with some boy in the woods by now.

"You're right." She sounded reluctant but agreed, glancing behind them nervously. "We should go."

"Come on." Still clutching her small hand in his, he led the way to his car. He'd loved the car before, but he was even happier now that he had his new, used convertible to impress Lizzie Barton with.

Chapter 2

Lizzie was working hard to control her breathing as she sat in the car next to Cole Ryan. Of all the ways she had imagined her birthday, this particular scenario hadn't occurred to her. She said a silent prayer of thank you that the sheriff had raided the party. That twist of fate had led her to where she was now, sitting next to Cole at the drive-in movie theater in his new car.

She tried not to hyperventilate as he laid one arm along the back of her seat, then let his fingers trail onto her shoulder. It was a classic timeless come-on move. She'd seen it in old movies. Before long, as she expected, his hand strayed down and ran up and down her arm.

She'd been afraid to hope that anything like this would happen with Cole. But when he'd put the convertible's top back up and parked way off to the side by the trees, she was pretty sure he was going to make a move on her during the movie.

Lizzie snuck a look at him and found him watching her. She blushed and he smiled. Embarrassed by the unexpected attention, she asked, "What?"

He shook his head. "Nothing. It's just, you've really grown up."

She steeled her nerves and went for it. Sitting up straighter in her seat and leaning closer to him, she said in her sexiest voice, "Yes, I have."

She watched him swallow as his eyes went wide. Perhaps she'd been too aggressive; she hadn't meant to frighten him off. Feeling a bit dejected, not to mention rejected, she started to back away from him. Then his hand found the back of her neck and pulled her head forward until their lips met.

Eyes closed, she practically saw fireworks against her eyelids from that kiss. She raised her hands out of her lap, wanting to touch him. Unsure exactly what to do with them, she rested them lightly on his chest and felt the hard muscles beneath his shirt.

Cole tilted his head and pushed his tongue between her lips and into her mouth. Lizzie wasn't exactly sure what to do with that, either. She'd played spin the bottle once or twice, but those had been barely pecks compared to this heavy-duty kiss. Trying to follow Cole's lead, she let his tongue explore the inside of her mouth and tried not to bite it by mistake. After a few minutes, she decided she really liked kissing, and leaned in even closer. Never in all her dreams had she imagined actually French-kissing Cole Ryan, but here she was.

He brought one hand up to her breast and squeezed through her t-shirt. She'd never understood the obsession boys had with boobs. Deciding it didn't bother her, she let him touch all he wanted, even when he slipped his hand under her shirt and bra and pinched her nipple. That hurt a little, but he seemed to really like it. Actually, she liked it, too and was starting to understand the whole boob obsession thing. Lizzie's lips were starting to feel swollen from all the kissing but she wasn't ready or willing to stop. Not even when Cole's hand strayed down to her bare leg. He ran it up and down against her skin until it inched its way up under her skirt, then between her thighs. She felt her own heart thundering so fast and loud, she was afraid he must feel and hear it, too. If he did, he didn't comment on it, but he did kiss her harder.

A boy had his hand up her skirt. She supposed she should care, but she didn't. She was enjoying it. Maybe she was acting like a slut, but she didn't care about that, either. She had been in love with Cole since she was a little girl. And now that she was legally a woman and he was actually showing an interest in her, she was willing to do whatever he wanted. So when he slid one finger under the elastic edge of her panties, she spread her legs further for him.

He groaned.

She was breathing heavier, partly with anticipation and a little bit with fear, when she felt his finger slide inside of her.

At that moment, she might have stopped breathing altogether. Thank goodness Cole stopped kissing her and she was able to breathe in and out of her mouth, because her nose wasn't doing it for her anymore. She was scared and nervous, but what he was doing felt good enough for her to totally ignore those other feelings.

He moved on to sticking his tongue in her ear while plunging his finger in and out of her fast, causing sensations she'd never felt before. She had no idea a finger could feel so good. She leaned her head and lifted her hips up off the seat and felt his finger slide deeper. A sound of pleasure escaped her throat that she couldn't stop. Cole echoed it with one of his own.

It was about then that she decided something that felt this good couldn't possibly be as bad to do as her parents said. She was enjoying what Cole was doing to her immensely when he suddenly stopped. She opened her eyes to see why and saw him struggling with his belt buckle in the dark of the car.

She swallowed. It was really going to happen. The bit *It*, with a capital 'I'. Trembling, she realized she wanted it to. Anna had done it long ago. Besides, she loved Cole. The first time should be with someone you loved. That's what everybody said.

She watched him unbutton his jeans and unzip the fly. Cole wore boxer shorts, which answered one of her life-long burning questions about him. That thought fled as he pushed the elastic waistband of his underwear down and she saw in the dim light *that* part of him.

He was breathing heavily, too, as he took her hand and placed it gently on his...she couldn't even think the word to her self. It was too embarrassing. Gathering enough nerve, she stroked it lightly, absolutely amazed at how something could be both so hard and feel so soft and silky at the same time. Touching the tip, she was surprised to find it slightly wet and slippery. She touched there again and slid her finger over the slit in the top.

She glanced at Cole's face and watched his eyes close as she stroked him. He blindly reached out a hand and found her again, sliding what felt like more than one finger inside her this time. He built a rhythm inside her and her breath caught in her throat as she trembled, her breath uncontrollable now.

She opened her eyes and found him watching her again. "Does this feel good?"

She nodded.

"Good." He smiled and moved slowly towards her, leaning over her.

Maneuvering an unseen lever, he sent her seat crashing back, leaving her practically horizontal, staring at the ceiling. Crawling over the center console, Cole kneeled on the seat between her spread legs and pushed her skirt up around her waist.

He began kissing her again, plunging his tongue in and out of her mouth as he pushed her underwear down. His fingers were soon replaced and she felt his hardness pressing against her. He rubbed himself over her again and again until she felt so sensitive down there she thought she might explode from just this contact with him.

Cole's breath was coming faster and, she realized, so was hers. His hips moved harder and faster until she felt the tip of him slip inside her. Her breath caught in her throat with surprise. He stilled and pulled away to look down at her face. "I'm sorry."

She shook her head. "It's OK. Really."

He got a strange, almost dreamy look on his face. His hips moved again, just a bit, nudging himself into her gently. He leaned over her and murmured against her ear, "Is this OK?"

She nodded, afraid she had no voice to answer.

He pushed against her again, harder this time, but it seemed he was too big or she was too small, because he didn't get any further than where he started.

Pulling away, she watched as he spit into his hand and

rubbed it onto himself, then onto her. Then he was over her again, whispering in her ear, "Relax."

It just figured! She couldn't even do this right. Cole must think she was such a loser. Afraid she would cry with disappointment and the fear of what he must be thinking about her, she squeezed her eyes closed just as she felt Cole rub himself in small circles against her, and then thrust forward and into her hard.

She gasped.

"You all right?" he breathed as he held himself still within her.

She managed to nod, not willing to admit to him that she felt stretched beyond limit, to the point of pain. Not thinking it was possible, he pushed deeper and she fisted her hands at her sides.

He started to move, pumping in and out of her more easily now. It wasn't as uncomfortable as it had been to begin with. In fact, it was feeling much nicer. She'd been a little scared there in the beginning, but now it actually felt good.

Cole made tiny sounds with each stroke, his breath tickling her ear. Knowing she was pleasing him made her even happier. But with her face pressed up against the cotton shirt covering his chest, she couldn't see him. She really wanted to see his face. When she'd dreamed of this moment, she'd pictured herself gazing into Cole's eyes, and he into hers. Then he would tell her he loved her...

"Lizzie."

Her heart leapt in her chest when he spoke her name. Maybe, just maybe...

"Yes, Cole."

"Are you on birth control pills?"

Lizzie's heart fell all the way down to the pit of her stomach. "No."

"That's OK. I'll pull out."

He pounded into her faster, and then yanked himself out of her with a grunt and a shudder, leaning heavily on shaking arms braced to either side of her. All too fast, he was making his way back into the driver's seat. She glanced up at the movie screen and saw the closing credits. She heard the sound of ignitions starting as cars around them flipped on their lights and began to move out of the lot.

That's it. Her first time was over. It seemed a bit of an anti-climatic ending to what was supposed to be such a monumental event in her life. She glanced at Cole. He was buckling his belt and looking very casual about it. That was it, then, she would just act casual, too.

Trying to ignore the warm wetness on the inside of her thighs, she adjusted her underwear and pulled her skirt back down over her thighs. After a moment of struggling with the seat back, she finally got it righted again, just as Cole started the car and drove out of the theater lot.

Lizzie was uncharacteristically silent during the trip from the drive-in to her house. Cole glanced at her. "You OK?"

She nodded and kept her face turned toward the side window.

Shit. He had let himself get carried away with her when he shouldn't have. Cole knew Lizzie had always had a schoolgirl crush on him. And until tonight, he'd always seen her as Bobby's little sister. It was just that she looked so different now, no longer a girl, but a woman. He'd forgotten she was still the same girl who'd followed him around googly-eyed.

He'd wanted her so badly, and she was so willing, he couldn't help himself. But it had still been wrong. He suddenly pulled the car over to the side of the road, threw it into park and turned in his seat toward her.

The crazy maneuver accomplished one thing. At least she looked at him. He reached out one hand and touched the side of her face. "You are not all right. I'm sorry, Lizzie. I moved too fast." He laughed bitterly. "I've been hanging around college girls too much. It's no excuse, I know, but I forgot for a minute how young you are."

Her eyes flashed with defiance. "I'm eighteen!"

And thank god for that, so at least it wasn't a felony. He shook his head at her and cupped her chin in his hand. "Just barely."

Then a horrible thought crossed his mind. "Oh, shit. Lizzie, you weren't a virgin, were you?"

A strange look crossed her face and she shook her head adamantly. "Of course not. I told you I'm not a baby. I'm an adult. Stop acting like Bobby."

And there was the other issue. Bobby, the most over-protective big brother you could ever meet *and* Cole's friend. Jeez, let your dick do the thinking for even a few minutes and look at all the trouble it could cause.

He sighed. He liked Lizzie, a lot. He always had. He'd just thought it had been only in a sisterly way. That was probably because he didn't have a sister of his own, he didn't know the difference. But tonight had proved that wasn't true, he liked her in a womanly way, too. And unlike the girls he'd been with at college, he didn't want to avoid her now that they'd had sex. He wanted her to stick around.

He sighed again. If only *he* could stick around.

"Liz, I have to leave for training camp soon. I barely have two days here and a ton of things to take care of in that time. What I'm saying is, I don't think I'll be able to see you again before I go."

She turned away from him again and faced the window, and judging by how deep she was breathing, he wouldn't be surprised if she was crying.

He touched her shoulder. "I want to see you again, Lizzie. Can I call you when I get there, or at least write to you while I'm gone? And maybe you could write to me, too." Why was he suddenly feeling so homesick about leaving a town he wanted nothing more to do with? Maybe it wasn't the town at all.

She turned back toward him with glassy eyes and a hopeful expression. "Do you really mean that? You actually would want me to write to you?"

He leaned in close and kissed her one cheek, and then the other. "Yeah. I'm sure lots of guys in the minor leagues have girlfriends at home."

"Girlfriend?" She smiled broadly at that.

He nodded and he kissed her sweet mouth. After a few more minutes of kissing, which only served to give him another hard-on, he pulled back. "Thank you."

"For what?"

"For tonight. For giving me something beautiful to remember while I'm alone in a strange city and missing home...and you."

Her face crumbled and she threw her arms around his neck. He heard her mumbled voice say against his shoulder, "You're welcome." Then he felt his shirt getting damp and knew for sure she was crying. At least this time, he figured they were happy tears.

They drove the rest of the way to Lizzie's house, made out for a bit more in the dark in her driveway, and then he left her with a promise to write her with his new address the moment he had it.

Cole was feeling good about the night, great actually, when he arrived home. In his room, he stripped off his clothes and threw them in the hamper, padding barefoot and naked to the bathroom. His was the only bedroom on the second floor, so privacy wasn't an issue, particularly at midnight when his parents were sound asleep.

Flipping on the light, he stood over the toilet, whose seat and lid were up, as usual. Then he looked down and froze when he saw the streaks of dried blood. That was all the evidence he needed to know that Lizzie had lied to him. She had been a virgin, until him.

His heart clenched. He'd actually asked her if she was on the pill. God, he was so stupid. Cole blew out a breath and felt like even more of an idiot bastard than he had before. And if Bobby somehow found out and beat the shit out of him for what he'd done to Lizzie, he'd accept it without a fight. He deserved it.

He braced his hands on the sink and hung his head. "Dammit, Lizzie. You should have told me."

Chapter 3
Present Day

The knot in Cole's stomach grew tighter the closer he neared Pigeon Hollow. He honestly never thought he'd be back there. Sure, maybe for a visit, but not to live. But his rotator cuff injury had seen to it that he was back for good. Nothing like losing twenty percent of the range of motion in your pitching arm to end a major league ballplayer's career.

He shook his head. Perhaps if he had admitted to the pain earlier on, the operation would have been more successful and he could have gotten back to one hundred percent. Hindsight was twenty-twenty, and he'd beat himself up about it everyday since the doctor and the physical therapist both told him this was as good as it was going to get. And then the team released him from his contract.

So here he drove, back to his parents and the town he'd left behind, in the same old convertible he'd left in ten years before. He'd been sentimental and kept it so long, the car had gone from just plain old to classic. As it turned out, it was a good thing he didn't blow all of his savings on overpriced sports cars, because the million dollar contracts were gone, along with his career.

He laughed bitterly at the reason why he'd kept the car. It was still hard to admit it was because this was where he'd made love to Lizzie. Lizzie, his sweet little girlfriend who had written him literally daily for about three weeks, then wrote him her last and final letter, saying goodbye for good.

He'd taken that rejection real well. First, he'd gone out and gotten stinking drunk. Then, he'd called her house in the middle of the night and demanded to know why she'd broken up with him. He badgered her until she was hysterical and Bobby had taken the phone away from her and hung up on him.

He vowed then and there while holding the handset of the payphone attached to the wall in the back of the bar to forget about Lizzie Barton. Besides, women were constantly throwing themselves at ballplayers. So when the next one did, he took her up on her offer. That hadn't worked out so well, though. The entire time he'd pounded himself into the stranger, he'd pictured Lizzie.

Yeah, he'd succeeded real well in getting her out of his mind. Even ten years later, he'd thought of nothing else but her the whole drive home. Well, maybe that wasn't entirely true. As the *Welcome to Pigeon Hollow* sign came into view, he did have one other thought besides Lizzie, and that was the realization that although he'd left this town a star, he was returning a big old loser.

~

Lizzie sat on the hard wooden bench and squinted into the sun, trying to distinguish the players on the field. The expected crowd was there, mostly parents cheering their kids on. In front of her were those one or two fathers who insisted on standing along the sidelines yelling advice to the players, even though it often contradicted that of the coaches.

The usual twinge of guilt twisted in Lizzie's gut at the fact that her son, Mikey, didn't have a father here for him. But then Lizzie reminded herself, as she so often did, who *was* cheering for Mikey. He had his Uncle Bobby and his Grandma and Grandpa Barton, and of course his mother, who loved him enough for two parents. So all in all, Mikey was probably the luckiest kid on the team.

She watched him step off the pitcher's mound, take off his cap and wipe the sweat off his brow with the back of his hand. The sun-bleached blond highlights of his hair glinted in the sun. She laughed to herself. Everyone with Barton blood had dark hair and blue eyes, except Mikey. Instead, he looked just like his father, with his hair the color of wheat and golden brown eyes. Didn't that just figure?

It always amazed her that the town hadn't figured out who his father was just by looking at him. The resemblance was so obvious to her. But no one had, so maybe it was her imagination. Of course, why should they suspect it was Cole Ryan? She'd never breathed a word of that one night to a soul, or even told anyone that she was writing to him everyday when he first went away. What they had together had been so precious to her, she hadn't wanted to share it with anyone, not even Anna. As it turned out, it was a good thing she hadn't.

Eventually, Bobby had guessed the truth, but that was only because he'd been there the night Cole called drunk and angry that she'd broken up with him by mail. But Bobby didn't judge her or reprimand her. In fact, they never discussed it again. Bobby had just accepted it and offered her silent support. He'd been there with money and a ride to the abortion clinic in the nearest city. And when she couldn't go through with it, he'd been there with a strong hand to hold when she told her parents she was pregnant but refused to name the father.

Bobby had been there for her then, and was still there for her now, acting as surrogate father to her son for things such as coaching little league games. There were just some things moms couldn't do, and this was one of them, as far as Mikey was concerned. She supposed 'the talk' would be another one of them, and that was probably only two or three years away now that Mikey was almost ten. God, he'd grown up so fast.

She shaded her eyes from the glare and watched Mikey powder his hands, get the feel of the ball and throw another strike. She had to smile. He had his father's pitching arm, too. Those Ryan genes sure were strong. There was barely even an ounce of Barton in Mikey. If she didn't know she'd given birth to him, she'd wonder if he was really hers.

At least she wouldn't have to worry about not being able to afford a good college for her son; she could practically see the baseball scholarships rolling in. But even so, she worked as many hours at the diner as she could to save up money. And living with her parents rent-free helped not only financially, but in the child-care department, too.

She'd made a good life for them both, even if she had given up her dream of going to college and becoming a teacher. Mikey would go to college for both of them.

Mikey, actually Mike—she'd have to remember he didn't like being called that any longer—struck out the batter and waited for the next one to take his place. In this level of little league, they weren't allowed to pitch an entire game, but Mike routinely retired every batter during his innings without allowing a single hit.

"Wow. That kid has some arm. Who does he belong to?"

She jumped nearly out of her skin. Although she may not have heard his voice in ten years, there was no mistaking it. She knew she would see him again some day, no avoiding it with his parents still in town, but she'd hoped it would be later rather than sooner. Guessing ten years was probably more reprieve than she should have expected, she turned and looked into the golden brown eyes of Cole Ryan.

She swallowed. "Hi."

"Hi, Lizzie." Tilting his head to look at her appraisingly, he smiled. "You look exactly as I remember you."

Her heart squeezed in her chest and she realized that even ten years hadn't erased her feelings for him. No wonder she'd never been able to seriously date anyone else, the teenager inside her still loved Cole Ryan. "Thanks. Um, you look great, too."

He laughed bitterly. "Yeah, thanks."

She couldn't help herself and reached out to touch his arm gently. "I heard about your injury, and your contract. I am so sorry."

He was a famous athlete, so it wasn't weird that she knew every detail of his career. He was a public figure, after all. It wasn't like she was obsessed or anything.

"Thanks," he said sincerely this time. "And so the star comes home a failure."

She frowned. "No one thinks that."

"Maybe you don't, but…"

"No. Seriously. I live here, Cole. I know. Everyone who knows you was very upset about your injury and pissed as hell that they would let you go because of it."

He smiled. "Can't blame them. Who needs a pitcher who can't pitch? And speaking of, you never told me whose kid that is."

She glanced out at the field and shrugged. "The pitcher? I'm not really sure."

He frowned at her. "Why are you sitting here in this sweltering heat watching a little league game, anyway?"

"Um. Bobby is a coach, so I, um, come to support him."

"Bobby is coaching? Does he have a kid playing?"

"Um, no."

He frowned at her again. "OK. Did he ever become the sheriff?"

Thanking god he'd changed the subject, she shook her head and smiled. "He's a deputy now, but it won't be long. One day he'll be sheriff." And just saying that one word, sheriff, flooded her with memories of the sheriff raiding the party in the woods, and what happened after.

Lizzie risked a glance at Cole's face and the expression she saw there told her he was thinking the same thing.

"Why did you do it, Lizzie? Why did you break up with me?"

Oh, boy. She never thought he'd come right out and ask after all these years. Why hadn't she rehearsed this particular scenario along with all of the others she'd imagined over the past ten years? "You needed to concentrate on your career. I was just a distraction."

He shook his head. "You were not. And besides, even if you had been, that was my decision to make, not yours."

"I handled it the wrong way. I'm sorry, Cole." She shrugged, trying to look like that decision hadn't ripped her heart out. "I was eighteen."

"I know exactly how old you were." He looked away, shaking his head angrily.

She bit her lip to stop herself, tasted blood and still asked anyway. "What do you want to say to me, Cole? Just say it."

He spun on her. "I guess I shouldn't have expected much from you since you've never told me the truth from the beginning anyhow."

Her heart pounded in her chest. Could he know? How? Her voice shook when she asked, "What are you talking about?"

He looked around to see who was in hearing range and lowered his voice to a hiss. "The fact that not only did you not tell me you were a virgin before I made love to you, but you lied about it after when I asked you point blank."

She breathed a sigh of relief. "Oh. That."

He raised a brow. "*Oh, that*? It mattered, you know."

"Why?"

"Because things would have been different. I would never have gone that far with you. At least not that night, not so soon."

She nearly laughed. Things would have been different, all right. He had no idea how true his words were.

Glancing back at the field, Lizzie noticed Mike retire the side and Bobby run up to talk to him. He had one more inning left to pitch and Bobby always made sure he wasn't too tired or hurting before he would let him go out to the mound again. For once, she wasn't worried about Mikey hurting himself playing ball. All she could think about now was how to get Cole as far away from Mikey as possible.

Cole glanced at Lizzie's profile as she watched the field and let out a big breath of frustration. Suddenly, he felt that he had to get away from her for a little while. How his disappointment could still be there after all this time was beyond him, but there it was, suspiciously feeling a lot like pain.

"I'm going over to say hi to Bobby."

"What? You can't!" Lizzie grabbed his arm in a claw-like death grip.

He frowned down at her hand. "Why not?"

"Because they're in the middle of a game, that's why not. You of all people should know better."

He raised his brow in shock. "I may be injured and no longer in the majors, but do you really think those kids don't

78

want some coaching advice from the formerly great Cole Ryan? Come on, Lizzie. What's really wrong with you?"

"Nothing's wrong with me."

"Then give me back my arm." What was this all about? Maybe she didn't want him to leave her? His heart leapt in his chest. Could she still care? "I promise, I'll come back and talk to you about us later, if that's what you want."

She dropped his arm like he'd suddenly electrocuted her. "That's not it. And there is no 'us'."

That took him aback. "Fine." He rolled his eyes at his own stupidity and stalked away toward the field.

Bobby was hanging onto the cage watching the hitter at bat when Cole came up behind him. "Need any coaching help from a former major leaguer?"

Cole's joke was answered by Bobby spinning around and punching him so hard, the next thing Cole knew, he was on his ass staring up at the sky. Then he could no longer see the sky, because the kids on both teams and most of the parents surrounded him.

Cole struggled to sit up and gingerly touched his jaw while looking up at Bobby's angry face. If he stood up now, Bobby would just punch him again, so he stayed where he was for the moment. He'd vowed ten years ago that if Bobby beat the crap out of him for taking Lizzie's virginity, he'd allow it. He just never imagined Bobby would come to collect ten years later. He guessed some offenses had no shelf life.

His train of thought was interrupted when the pitcher he'd admired from the bleachers broke through the crowd and said, "Uncle Bobby! Why did you punch him?"

With his mind still working a little slowly from the punch, Cole took a moment to wonder why Lizzie said she didn't know who he was if he was her and Bobby's nephew. The kid must be her sister Mary Sue's son, so why would Lizzie lie?

It was a good thing that Cole remained sitting on the ground, because what he heard next would have knocked him on his ass again otherwise. "Mom! Get him some ice out of the cooler!" And when Cole looked to see *Mom*, she turned out to be Lizzie.

Head still spinning, he stared at the boy and realized he looked nothing like his mother and everything like Cole himself. He took a shaky breath and asked him the question he feared the answer to most. "You've got some pitching arm on you, boy. How old are you anyway?"

The boy smiled proudly. "I'll be ten in February, sir."

Ten. The magic number. Cole swallowed as acid backed up his throat.

Lizzie was suddenly beside them both. "Mike, go find your grandparents."

Mike? At that, Cole finally got to his feet and looked Lizzie right in the eye. "You named him after my father? Is that supposed to make up for keeping this a secret from me for ten damn years?"

Bobby's eyes opened wide. "Lizzie! He didn't know?"

Lizzie looked panicked. "Mikey, I need you to come away from here now." She looked behind her for her parents, who Cole hadn't noticed before. "Mom, Dad. Please, take Mikey home. Now."

"Mom. The game's not done yet. Please don't make me go." Mikey pleaded with his mother as his grandparents ushered him briskly off the field.

Cole turned back to Lizzie and spotted a television camera barely ten feet away from him. "How the fu..." He hardly managed to censor his language in front of the rest of the kids in time. He closed his eyes to gain his composure. "How did reporters find me here already?"

Bobby looked back at the camera and groaned. "They're not reporters. I'll take care of it." He started to head for the camera crew, stopped and turned back to Cole. "Don't go anywhere."

"Why? You gonna hit me again?"

"No, I'm gonna apologize and Lizzie's gonna explain."

Cole cocked his head carelessly. "In that case, I'll wait."

While Bobby went to have a very animated argument with a little brunette and the cameraman, Cole turned back to Lizzie. Thankfully, the other coaches and parents had somehow gotten the game back on track, so at least the audience was gone. Cole felt free to voice his opinion to Lizzie about the sudden turn of events. "I can't believe you would do something like this. You had no right."

"I had every right. He's my son."

"He's *our* son."

She frowned and folded her arms across her chest. "You don't know that."

Cole laughed. "Come on, Lizzie. It's like looking in a goddamn mirror. Besides, your brother wouldn't have attacked me like that unless he thought I was Mikey's father." He reached out and gripped her by both arms. "Why the hell didn't you tell me?"

Tears filled her eyes and spilled down her cheeks unchecked as she shook her head, but she didn't answer.

Suddenly, Bobby was back beside him. "OK. I got rid of them but only for a little while. I'm going to have to sell my soul for that damn tape. But at least we can get out of here and talk in private."

Cole had no clue what Bobby was talking about, but at the moment, he didn't care. "We've got it covered, Bobby. Lizzie and I can handle this alone."

Bobby shook his head. "Nuh, uh. You're angry and you've got Lizzie cryin' now. I can't let you be alone with her."

Cole sighed and let his arms drop from Lizzie's. "Fine. Come along. I don't care."

Lizzie shook her head, still crying. "You two can both go to hell for all I care, but I'm not comin' along." And with that she spun on her heel and ran off the field.

Bobby sighed and shook his head, watching her go. "We're probably better off, anyway. You and I will get things squared away between us, then we'll deal with her later."

Cole nodded. "Can we do it over a stiff drink and an ice pack?"

Bobby laughed, "Sure thing."

So there Cole sat, opposite Bobby in the dimly-lit bar next to The Hideaway, literally hiding from the half a dozen television camera crews roaming the town. "I can't believe that in this friggin' hole-in-the-wall town, a man has to hide from television cameras!"

"Yeah, and the head producer decided I was going to be a 'main character', so they're on me eighteen hours a day, if not more."

Cole shook his head. "Well, the timing sucks."

"I know. I'm sorry, but we've all signed releases and can't get out of them. Just don't you sign one now that you're back. Maybe I'll be able to keep you out of this damn reality TV show."

Cole shook his head. "They don't need a release. I'm a public figure, my life is public domain."

"Shit."

"Exactly," Cole echoed Bobby's sentiments and raised his glass.

"About Lizzie and Mike. I thought you always knew and just didn't give a shit. I never imagined she didn't tell you." Bobby nursed his sore hand by keeping it shoved in the bucket of ice supplied by the bored-looking day shift bartender.

Cole laughed bitterly while holding a cold pack on his own sore jaw. "If I'd known, Bobby, I would have married her and moved her to the city to be with me. You know me better than that."

"I thought I did, but then again, I never knew you were sleepin' with my sister." Bobby downed another slug of his drink. "And why the hell didn't you two use birth control?"

"It was only the one time, and I pulled out."

"Yeah, well, that didn't work out too well, now did it?"

"No. Believe me, I know better now. But I swear, Bobby, I was serious about Lizzie. I wanted a relationship with her, even if it had to be long distance in the beginning. Then she went and dumped me. No reason, no explanation, in a goddamn letter."

"That must have been when she figured out she was pregnant."

"But why not tell me?"

Bobby shrugged. "Don't know. That's somethin' you'll have to ask her, if you can get her cornered."

"Yeah, easier said than done." Cole fiddled with his glass, and then asked the question he'd been wanting to since they'd arrived. "What's he like?"

Bobby broke into a grin. "I couldn't be prouder of him if he were my own."

Envy ate at his gut. "I wish I'd gotten to see him grow up."

"I know, and I'm sorry about that. But hey, you're here now. The first few years they don't do much more than sleep and shit, anyway. Now is when we're gettin' into the good stuff," Bobby reasoned.

Cole nodded. "Yup. And for the first time since my injury, I am happy I'm off the team. I'm gonna get to know him, Bobby. I'm going to publicly claim him as mine. Hell, I'll get my own place and he can stay with me if he wants."

"Whoa, wait a minute there. Mike lives in the Barton house and has since the day he was born."

"Things can change."

All of a sudden, Bobby's hand was on Cole's arm. "A word of advice. Start slow. Don't piss off Lizzie, and don't make big waves in the kid's life or Lizzie's. I don't think she can take it."

"I'm not out to hurt anybody, but I want him to know me."

"He already idolizes the public you. He was glued to the television for every game you played just because he knew you grew up in this town and he wanted to be like you. All you need to do now is let him get to know the private you. Hell, what kid wouldn't want the great Cole Ryan as his daddy?"

Cole had to smile. "He inherited my arm."

"I've noticed." Bobby laughed.

Cole took a sip from his glass slowly so not to jar his tender jaw and then shook his head. "It's a lot to take in."

Bobby inclined his head in a nod. "Yup."

"I've got to introduce him to my parents. He's got another whole set of grandparents he knows nothing about."

Bobby nodded again.

"I should probably tell my parents first, and then bring Mikey over."

"He doesn't like being called Mikey anymore. Now that he's almost ten, he wants to be *Mike*." Bobby informed him with a smile.

Cole raised a brow. "Oh, thanks for telling me. Although, it may get confusing when he and my father are in the same room." He was feeling bitter and confused again. She'd named Mike after his father, but still never told him his son even existed.

As if reading his mind, Bobby said, "She's never stopped thinkin' about you, you know. It really pissed me off when I thought you were a deadbeat shit-head, but she keeps a scrapbook of everythin' she could find concernin' you."

Cole snorted. "Well, that's nice, but I would have rather she told me about Mike."

"There's plenty of photo albums and scrapbooks of Mike that I'm pretty sure she made for you. Hell, we've got the real thing underfoot, she didn't need to make 'em for us."

Pictures. Yeah, *that* would make up for missing nearly ten years of his son's life. Cole took a deep breath and then stood, unable to sit still any longer. "I gotta go."

Bobby raised a brow. "Lizzie?"

He shook his head. "No. My parents, before the town gossip reaches them. You're right. I'm still too angry to see Lizzie quite yet. Nothing productive will come out of talking to her like this."

Bobby nodded his approval and then handed him a

sheriff's department card. "Call me on my cell if you want me to bring Mike over to your parents, or if you just need to talk. But I gotta warn you. For the next few weeks, I come with a camera up my ass."

Cole sighed. "Great. My timing always was impeccable."

Chapter 4

Lizzie sat in the kitchen of the Barton house and ran her finger up and down the condensation on her glass of iced tea. She was still in her waitress uniform from the late shift at the diner and she smelled like grease and dirty dishrags, but she didn't care. At the moment, she didn't have the mental or physical energy to go change or shower.

It had been one hell of a shift. In addition to the camera crew that had parked itself in the diner for the evening rush, the news about Cole had circulated through town faster than a fire through dry brush. There was more whispered gossip than usual in Pigeon Hollow, and the expected sudden silence whenever she neared.

Lizzie let out a loud breath. It was good to be home.

She usually enjoyed the quiet of coming home after the late shift, but not tonight. Bobby was out bowling. Her parents and Mikey were all sleeping. And she was left listening to her own conscience shout accusations at her. Well-deserved accusations, and that was what sucked most.

She'd robbed Cole of nearly ten years of his son's life, and now she was going to pay for it. He was rich, he was famous, and he was pissed off at her. In a custody battle, he would win, no doubt, and she would lose the only thing she had in life that mattered to her.

She lifted the iced tea glass and was just using the paper napkin underneath to wipe the tears streaming down her cheeks when she heard the screen door open. She turned, expecting to see Bobby, but instead found Cole.

He strode over to her side and knelt on the floor by her feet. Raising one hand to her cheek, he brushed a tear away. "Don't."

His being sweet was exactly what she didn't expect and it broke what little composure she had left. She was a weepy sobbing mess in an instant as Cole pulled her into his arms and tried to comfort her.

What started out as comfort, turned into something else.

86

He kissed the tears from her face until he reached her mouth, lingered there and then suddenly pulled away.

"I'm sorry." He shook his head, as if disappointed in his own behavior. Although, honestly, kissing him had felt good, bone-deep good. "I've thought about kissing you every day for the last ten years," Cole admitted.

Lizzie closed her eyes and took in that information. "Cole."

He put one finger on her lips. "Don't. Don't say anything if you're going to tell me to leave, or remind me that it's over between us."

"What do you want to do?" She couldn't wait any longer to ask about the situation with Mikey. Cole didn't seem so angry any more. Perhaps he wouldn't sue her for custody, but she was sure he would want something.

He raised a brow at her question and cocked his head to one side, letting his hand linger on her knee. She realized exactly what he was inferring. "Cole! That's not what I was talking about."

He smiled. "Can't blame me for trying. And at least you're smiling now."

She sighed. "Yeah. But still, we need to talk."

He nodded. "You're right." He rose from his knees and sat in the kitchen chair opposite hers. Taking a sip of her iced tea, he placed the glass back between them. "I want to be a part of his life, Liz, as his father."

"OK. You deserve that at least."

"Have you told him yet?"

"No." She'd managed to avoid that conversation and his questions so far. Working at the diner had at least been good for one thing that night.

"Good. I'll be back in the morning and we'll tell him together. OK?"

She swallowed hard and nodded.

"What time should I come by?"

She shrugged. "We all get up pretty early, but since it's summer, Mikey doesn't have school. Anytime after eight, I guess."

He nodded. "Unless of course, you invite me to stay the night?" He raised a brow hopefully.

Lizzie felt herself blush. "Cole!"

He grinned at her, and stood. Leaning down to kiss her lips gently, he said, "I want my son in my life, Lizzie. But I also want my son's mother. Remember that."

That comment nearly stopped her heart right in her chest.

He turned to leave, but then looked back. "Why are you wearing that horrible outfit?"

She giggled. "It's my uniform. But thanks for the compliment."

He frowned. "Uniform for what?"

"I waitress at the diner."

"Why?" He inched back closer and towered over her.

"Because I have no skills to get a better job and I have to save for Mikey's future. That's why, Mr. Hot Shot Ballplayer."

"There is no need for you to work there. I want you to quit that job tomorrow."

"First of all, I can't just up and quit. Mac is overwhelmed as it is with all the extra business from the TV crew. Second, I like it there and I make good tips. And third, you have no right to tell me what to do." Tired of him standing over her, she stood now, too.

His frown deepened. "First of all, it sure as hell is my business what you do. You're the mother of my child. Second, I will support both you and Mikey financially, including paying for college, so you don't have to work there or anywhere else for that matter. And third, Mac can take his diner and shove it. It is not your problem to staff it!"

In the midst of the arguing, Lizzie didn't notice Bobby arrive until he opened the screen door and was half through. He took one look at the two of them sparring nose to nose, spun on his heel and shoved the ever-present cameraman back out the door by his lens. "How about we hit The

Hideaway for a bit, boys and girls? I bet we can find you some nice drunks that will make mighty good TV."

She and Cole were silent until the trio were out of the driveway, then Cole spoke. "I'm calling my lawyer first thing in the morning."

Lizzie's heart was in her throat. "No, Cole. Please, don't. I'll quit my job. I'll do anything you want me to. Just don't take him away from me." Her last words came out in a sob.

Cole stepped forward and grabbed her by both arms. "What are you talking about?"

"You're mad a me, so you're going to try to take Mike away."

Cole scowled and shook his head. "No, Lizzie. I'm calling my lawyer because I want to change my will to name Mike and set up a trust for him. But if that is what you really think of me, then we have more problems than I thought." He laughed bitterly. "So much for my plans for creating a happy family."

Then he was gone, and she was left alone with her guilt and her fears.

~

It's amazing how things work out sometimes. One moment, life could be great and you're thinking you may actually get everything you've ever wanted. Then the next, just a split second later, nothing is the same.

That scenario seemed to be happening to Cole a lot lately. There was the meteoric rise, followed by the ultimate crash and burn fall of his baseball career. Then there was the mind-blowing discovery that he had a son by the very woman he couldn't get out of his mind, followed shortly by the discovery that she didn't know him or trust him. Not one tiny bit.

If Lizzie could believe he was the kind of man who would try to take their son away from his mother, then they had no hope of a future together.

Future. Yeah, that was the other thing currently weighing down his already overloaded mind. Lizzie had no future thanks to him. Cole had come to that disconcerting realization last night after seeing her in that horrid black and white polyester waitress uniform. Lizzie had given up her college scholarship and her dreams of becoming a teacher to have his baby. Waiting tables instead of teaching, that didn't make him feel *too* shitty.

Of course she couldn't have gone to college. How could she have lived in the dorms as an unmarried, pregnant freshman in her second trimester? And since then, she'd been raising his son and trying to make enough to pay for his future by slinging greasy food.

Cole shook his head. She'd been stupid not to tell him, or maybe brave. Probably a little of both. There were women he'd come across in the pros who tried to get pregnant with a ballplayer's baby, just so they could take him for all he was worth. And here was Lizzie, hiding it from him for years and wanting nothing now. He supposed he should respect that, but all he wanted to do was shake some sense into her so she'd let him take care of them both.

The morning sun was already high in the sky as he stood at the Bartons' back door. Cole took a deep breath. He was facing not only his son, but also Lizzie's parents for the first time since the great ball field revelation yesterday. They definitely weren't going to be too happy with him.

He knocked on the wooden frame of the screen door, something he hadn't done the night before when he'd seen Lizzie alone and crying in the kitchen.

Mikey ran to the door, half a corn muffin in his hand. "Mr. Ryan! Mom said you were going to stop by, but I didn't believe her. Did you really used to play ball with Uncle Bobby? How's your chin where he punched you? Does it hurt? What was it like to pitch in the World Series? Do you want breakfast? There's plenty."

Cole smiled at his son. *His son.* He'd have to get used to that. Suddenly, in the face of Mikey's pre-pubescent ramblings, he wasn't quite so nervous anymore. "Thanks, Mikey. I'm good. But I wouldn't mind some coffee if it's made."

"Sure, I'll run and get you a mug!"

Mikey ran to the pantry off the side of the kitchen and climbed like a monkey onto the counter to reach the high mug cabinet. Cole stepped further into the kitchen and took in the sight of all four adult Bartons sitting around the table, watching him intently.

He inclined his head to Lizzie's parents. "Ma'am, Sir. I know we need to talk. Later, in private. I owe you both an explanation."

Mr. Barton stood, equaling Cole's own six foot one inch frame. Cole wouldn't have been surprised if the man clocked him one, too, just like Bobby had.

Instead, he extended his hand. "No need, son. Lizzie explained it all. The missus and I are going to get out of here so you two can explain it to Mike."

Cole nodded. "Thank you. I appreciate that. But before you go, would you mind witnessing this? That's why I'm late. I had to wait for my lawyer to fax it. It's my will, leaving everything to Mikey, except for a small trust to take care of my parents in case I go before they do."

Mr. Barton took the paper in his hand and swallowed. "Sure, son." He turned to find a pen and Cole saw tears shining in Mrs. Barton's eyes.

He'd spent a lot of time in this kitchen growing up. The Bartons had been like a second set of parents to him, and to have their understanding meant everything to him.

After the surprisingly emotional signing of the will, Lizzie's parents left, followed immediately by Bobby, who mumbled something about getting out before the crew arrived. Suddenly, Cole's new family unit of three were alone.

Cole sat at the large kitchen table opposite Mikey and Lizzie and gripped the coffee mug tightly in his hand.

Mikey looked from him to his mother. "Am I in trouble or something?"

Cole and Lizzie both jumped to tell him no.

Mikey pivoted from one face to the other, looking confused. "Then why did Grandma, Grandpa and Uncle Bobby leave? And why do you both look so serious?"

Cole swallowed. "Mikey...I mean Mike."

Mikey smiled. "It's OK, Mr. Ryan. You can call me Mikey if you want."

Cole was aware of Lizzie raising her brow at that, but ignored it. "Thanks, Mikey. I will. Now." Cole blew out a breath and dove right in. "What has your mother told you about your father?"

Mikey shrugged. "She said that not every kid has a dad. I know that. Lots of kids don't. There is even a kid at school whose cousin in New York has two moms and no dad."

Cole bit his lip to stop from smiling at that. He was just thinking how to proceed when Mikey continued.

"Of course, you need a dad's sperm to have a baby."

Lizzie choked on the swallow of coffee she had just taken and Cole felt himself blanch. Well, he'd wanted to be a real father to Mikey, for better or worse. Discussing the birds and the bees was about as fatherly as it got.

Cole nodded. "You are absolutely right about that, Mikey. Um, I'm just wondering, where exactly did you hear about sperm?"

Mikey shrugged again. "Everybody knows about *that*."

"Oh. OK. Well. I'm glad we can speak as adults here, then."

Mikey looked very solemn and nodded. "Yes, sir. We can."

Cole restrained his smile. This kid was full of surprises. "Good. Now, do you know whose sperm your mom used when she decided to have you?" Cole could only hope that Mikey was picturing test tubes and lab scientists when he spoke of sperm and making babies.

Mikey frowned and looked at his mother, then back to Cole. "No. I guess I never thought to ask."

"Well Mikey, your mom used my sperm to make you, which makes me your father. I didn't know about it at the time. That's why we've never met until now. But I want you to know that I'm very happy now that I know about you."

"You're my dad? Cole Ryan is my dad!" Mikey leapt from his chair, whooped and jumped in a circle in the middle of the kitchen. Then he stopped. "This isn't some kind of joke or something, is it?" He looked at Lizzie.

"No, it's not a joke. Mr. Ryan is your father."

Mikey's face lit up again and broke into a huge grin.

"And you can't keep calling me Mr. Ryan."

"What should I call you then?" Mikey asked, quite logically.

"Whatever you decide is fine with me." He didn't dare suggest Dad so soon, even though nothing would please him more.

Mikey hesitated for a moment. "Can I think about it?"

Cole forced a smile, hiding his disappointment. "Sure. And I want you to know, that although I wasn't around before, I'm going to make up for it now. OK with you?"

He smiled and nodded. "OK. Will you coach me on my pitching?"

Cole laughed. "Just try and stop me."

Mikey ran over and hugged first his mother, then Cole. "This is so great! Can I go call all my friends?"

Lizzie, teary eyed, nodded. "Sure."

Teary eyed himself after that hug, Cole watched his son run from the room and then, for the first time in he didn't know how many minutes, he breathed freely.

They both sat silently for a while, recovering from the emotional revelation.

"You handled that really well." Lizzie looked at him with a sincerity that choked him up even more.

"Thanks." He blew out a big breath. "That was both much easier and much harder than I thought it would be."

Lizzie laughed. "I know what you mean."

Cole gazed into his coffee mug and asked the question he was afraid to ask even himself. "Do you think he would have been so excited if I wasn't *the* Cole Ryan?"

Lizzie considered for a second. "I think that although I've done everything I could to make sure he's had positive male role models in his life, no one can make up for not having a father. So, maybe he wouldn't have danced around the kitchen, but he still would have been happy to have you, even if you weren't *the* Cole Ryan."

"Thanks, Lizzie."

"Please don't thank me, Cole." She looked pained.

He covered her hand with his, and then changed the subject. They were both too emotional to get involved in the 'why didn't you tell me ten years ago' discussion. He moved them both into safer waters. "Do you have a copy of his baseball schedule?"

She nodded and got up to get it for him. It was taped to the inside of the kitchen cabinet, the same place it had been taped when he and Bobby played ball when they were Mikey's age. Some things never changed, and he was glad of it.

"You did right, Lizzie. Keeping him here with your parents. It's a good place to grow up." Before he got sentimental all over again, he retreated. "So, when do you think I should bring him to meet my parents?"

She laughed. "He's seems to be handling this better than us, so whenever you want, I guess. How did they take it?"

Cole shrugged. His parents had been thrilled. It seemed he and Lizzie were the only two having issues with this situation. "Fine. Apparently grandchildren are always welcome, doesn't really matter how they appear."

She smiled at him. "Good. I'm glad. You know, I tried to never get gas at your parents' station with Mikey in the car because I was afraid they'd see the resemblance."

He fingered the paper folded in his pocket and shook his head at her. "Lizzie. Are you really worried I'd take him away from you?"

Lizzie looked pained. "He's all I've got, Cole."

Cole sighed. He pulled out the paper and unfolded it on the table in front of her. "I had my lawyer draw this up, too."

When she looked panicked, he quickly explained. "It says I will never seek custody of Mike."

Cole got up and retrieved the pen Mr. Barton had left on the counter. He sat and pulled the paper toward him when Lizzie covered his hand. "No. You don't need to sign that. I know in my heart that you would never take him away from me. But you have to understand, losing a child in any capacity is every mother's worst fear."

"Then let me sign it and you'll have one less thing to worry about."

She shook her head. "No. I trust you." She folded the paper again and handed it to him, unsigned.

He took it and put it away in his pocket, hoping this meant things might actually be looking up with Lizzie. He'd come home to Pigeon Hollow a broken man. But through Mikey, Lizzie had given him the gift of a future again. Ten years late, but better late then never.

Chapter 5

Cole started making good on his promise to Mikey to be around as much as possible that very night, which is what led to Lizzie sitting once again in the passenger seat of his convertible at the drive-in. The only difference between this time and ten years ago was Mikey, seated in the back seat. Well, Mikey *and* the fact that Cole and she weren't... She pushed that memory away.

Lizzie thanked god for Mikey's presence to break the tension, but it wasn't meant to last. He saw some friends, begged to go to the snack bar with them, jumped out of the back seat and was gone.

Then she was alone with Cole. Again. He glanced at her. "You all right?"

"Yeah, I'm fine." Lizzie forced a smile and tried to look fine.

He rubbed her shoulder and she felt herself stiffen. "This was a bad idea. I should sell this car." He shook his head and looked very serious as he said it, pulling his hand away from her.

Laughing, Lizzie reached out and squeezed his arm. "You don't have to sell the car. Yeah, it's a little weird, even after all this time, but I really am fine."

He shook his head. "It doesn't feel like ten years. It feels like yesterday."

"I know."

Cole turned in the seat and faced her, like he had so many years ago. "I need you to know that I still want to be with you as much as I did then, Lizzie. Maybe more. I never stopped."

She swallowed and bit her lip. "Mike's on his way back. We'll talk about this later."

Cole cocked a brow as if saying they'd do a lot more than talk if it were up to him. She had a lot to think about, including her heart and body, who betrayed her brain at every turn when it came to Cole Ryan.

They only stayed for the first movie and then left. If the second movie in the double feature hadn't been an R-rated bloody horror flick, she would have suggested they stay for that too, just to avoid going home and being alone with Cole for their 'talk' about how he wanted them to be together.

Mikey had already had more than enough junk food meaning they couldn't even go out for ice cream, her other idea to stall. The inevitable discussion, which would probably entail him asking once again why she kept Mikey a secret from him, was something she would happily avoid completely if possible.

So with a sleeping Mikey in the back seat, they had driven directly home. And now, there she was, alone with Cole on the porch, in the swing no less. Why she agreed when he suggested this inherently romantic setting, she had no idea.

She was confused and frightened and hopeful all at the same time. She thought she wanted to be with him, as a family, but she didn't want him if he only wanted to be with her because of Mikey.

The problem was, when she was near him like this, her brain turned to mush and she couldn't think at all.

Cole sat beside her, swinging them gently with his long legs while staring out into the dark. The typical sounds of a southern summer night surrounded them, but he remained quiet, something for which she should be immensely grateful. Although, the anticipation of the talk about their future was worse than just getting it over with.

He laid one arm along the back of the swing and pulled her closer. Her heart quickened and she had trouble keeping her breath even. Tilting his head, he leaned it against hers, but still remained quiet.

This felt both too natural and unnatural at the same time. Sure, she had been in love with him since she was old enough to realize girls were supposed to like boys. And yeah, they shared a child. However, they had shared barely a handful of kisses and only one night together, along with an absence from each other of ten long years.

Finally, she couldn't take any more of the silence she had so wished for. "Cole. What do you want from me?" she murmured, unable to control herself.

She felt him kiss the top of her head. "Exactly this."

Lizzie raised a brow. "And…"

He laughed. "When did you get so cynical and suspicious? Lizzie, our son is sleeping inside after I got to spend the whole evening with him, and now you are in my arms. It's a perfect night."

"And you want nothing else from me?"

He laughed. "Maybe you are right to be suspicious. I do want something else from you." He bent his head and brushed his lips lightly across hers.

Her eyes drifted shut, but when he ended the kiss much too soon, she opened them again. Looking at him, she was torn between wanting more and wanting to run away. Smiling at her, he kissed her again, not so lightly this time.

A long time and many kisses later, she realized she'd inched closer until they were pressed together in spite of the heat, and she was hot enough to give him anything he wanted from her. What was it about Cole Ryan that turned her into a teenager? Twenty-eight years old and necking on the front porch while her parents slept inside. Honestly!

She leaned even closer, his hands so tantalizingly near her breasts, but still not touching them. Then his touch suddenly disappeared. Breaking the kiss, he stood unexpectedly, sending a quiver through both the chains suspending the swing and her.

Cole leaned down and cupped her face one last time. He kissed her chastely on the lips and then walked to the edge of the porch. "I'll see you in the morning. We can drive to the game together."

Then he was gone, leaving her in shocked silence.

~

Cole had walked away from Lizzie, smiling and suffering at the same time. He'd left her on the porch wanting him, of that he was sure. As sure as he was of the raging hard-on she'd left him with. For some reason she was still fighting the obvious, that they should be together as a couple and as a family. But it was worth the abstinence if it convinced her she couldn't live without him, even though it was nearly killing him. This playing hard to get was, quite frankly, hard.

As he arrived back at the Barton's in time for breakfast the next morning, Cole realized his being there at bedtime and then back again by breakfast was almost like living together, without the all-important aspect of sex with Lizzie, of course. Perhaps he'd be able to remedy that part soon, before he exploded, and not in a good way.

Mikey greeted him with his usual overwhelming enthusiasm, the Bartons with parental affection, and Lizzie with forced airiness. Bobby barely greeted him at all as he flew out of the screen door when the camera crew pulled into the drive. Maybe after this Lizzie mess was settled, he'd get around to finding out how Hollywood had come to invade Pigeon Hollow. But right now, he had other things to worry about, like Mikey's pitching and how his teammates would react to Cole's presence as his long lost father at the game today.

Hmm, his so-called *problems* had taken on a whole new look now that he was back in Pigeon Hollow. If the most he had to worry about was how his son pitched today and how he was going to get Lizzie into bed, he was doing pretty damn good.

As it turned out, Cole needn't have worried about Mikey. He was amazing. Mikey pitched a no-hitter, at least for his half of the game. With Cole's coaching, the relief pitcher only gave up a few hits during the game's last half and Mikey's team won easily.

And as far as the other kids accepting him as Mikey's father, Cole felt like a bigger star being Mikey's dad than he ever had being a major league pitcher. It was a really good feeling. He may no longer be in the pros, but he would always be Mikey's dad.

He suddenly understood Lizzie's fear that he would take Mikey away. It would hurt Cole to lose Mikey even after just a few days of knowing him. He could only imagine what Lizzie felt since she'd carried him inside her for nine months. Nine months he wasn't allowed to share with her. The anger was still present, squashed away there in the background, as well as the questions. Hopefully, he'd find the resolutions for both soon.

It was with that goal in mind that Cole slipped twenty bucks into Bobby's palm and quietly suggested he take the team out for ice cream after the game. The senior Barton members had already left for an afternoon church service, so that left Cole, Lizzie and an empty house.

Whether it was physical or emotional, he didn't care, but Cole intended on finding some sort of release with Lizzie today. He'd waited too long for her already. Too long to hold her in his arms again. Too long for answers to his many questions. He was done waiting.

Chapter 6

Lizzie was alone with Cole in the house. How the hell had that happened in a home where five people lived together? Usually they were on top of each other, waiting for the shower or literally stepping on each other in the crowded kitchen.

She'd hoped it would be safe to accept the ride home Cole offered because it was still daylight, but judging by the look in Cole's eyes, neither the position of the sun nor the time on the wall clock mattered. He was looking like a very handsome, not to mention firm-bodied predator, and she felt very much like prey.

Her mouth suddenly dry, she swallowed and offered Cole a glass of iced tea. When all else fails, resort to good old southern hospitality. He accepted the offer of iced tea, although she probably could have offered him cyanide and his answer wouldn't have been any different. It clearly wasn't the tea he was after.

Facing the cold air of the open fridge, she felt him step close behind her. She realized turning her back on him was a mistake, right up there in magnitude with being alone with him in the empty house.

Doing a little sidestep dance, she managed to get both herself and the plastic pitcher out of the fridge and shut the door. She put a bit of distance between them by walking to the pantry to get two glasses. Big mistake there, too, because when he followed her, she had nowhere to sidestep.

She put the pitcher down on the counter, crossed her arms over her chest and stared him boldly in the eye. "What are you up to?" She hadn't been expecting a good answer, but she'd thought she'd get at least something.

Actually, she did get something all right, his mouth covering hers, followed quickly by his tongue. And in answer, her traitorous mouth responded and her tongue met his. Her arms didn't stay crossed long, and before she could stop them, they were wrapped around the back of Cole's head, pulling him closer even as his hands pulled her hips closer to him.

He lifted her and sat her on the counter so he wouldn't have to bend to reach her mouth. He stepped easily between her legs. "I've never stopped thinking about you, wanting you."

He moved on to teasing the whorls of her ear with his tongue and she melted against him. Figuring she could keep trying to deny that she'd never stopped wanting him either, or just enjoy this, she made the obvious decision. "Me, too."

He pulled back and looked at her with eyes barely focused. Then crashed back into her with a powerfully possessive kiss that she enjoyed the feel of way too much.

Her hands crept beneath his t-shirt and she remembered the hard feel of his body. Copying her, he slid his hands beneath her tank top and didn't stop until they divested her of her bra and found her nipples.

He groaned and broke away again. "Not here. I want to do this right this time, Lizzie. I've waited too long to make it right to screw up again now." He pulled her toward him, her legs wrapped around his back, then carried her all the way to her bedroom at the other end of the house.

Depositing her on the bed, he flipped on the window air conditioner to cool the near stifling room, then closed the door to the hall. When he stood in front of her and stripped naked, she finally saw him in all his glory. They may have made a baby together, but she'd never actually seen him naked. He was quite a tempting sight.

He knelt on the bed, unashamed, and began to slowly undress her next. Being summer, there weren't many clothes to remove, so it didn't take all that long before she was naked, too, and trembling. She'd never seen him naked, but far more importantly; he had never seen her, either. She was nervous about that. She wasn't eighteen anymore. He didn't seem to care.

Cole lay down next to her and ran kisses up and down her body. "You are so beautiful."

She blushed and shook her head. "I've had a baby. Things tend to move around and never go back." As she said that, she tried to support her sideways sliding boobs by squeezing her arms closer to her sides.

Smiling at her, he shook his head. "No. You are beautiful. Every inch." He took one nipple in his mouth, apparently not caring what breastfeeding Mikey had done to her former perkiness.

Lizzie pressed her head further back against the pillow and closed her eyes, enjoying Cole's touch a hell of a lot more now than she had ten years before. She wasn't sure if he had gotten better, or if she'd just gotten older, but she was pretty sure that making love to the adult Cole would be nothing like it had been with the teenage Cole.

He worked his way down her body, until he finally slid his hands between her thighs. His mouth soon followed his hands. Shocked at what he could make her feel, she cried out as he worked until wave upon wave of an incredible orgasm struck her. She was absolutely correct in her prediction, adult Cole knew what he was doing, and adult Lizzie, not having been with anyone in a very, very long time, appreciated it.

She was breathless when she finally grabbed his head and pulled him up. Level with her, he stroked her face, then shook his head. "I wasn't very good that first time, was I?"

Lizzie smiled. "Don't worry. You more than made up for it now, and I was too young to know any better then anyway."

"I plan on spending the rest of my life making it up to you, Lizzie."

Her eyes opened wide. He couldn't be asking her *that*. Could he? "Cole…"

"Shhh. Later." He shook his head and covered her mouth with his.

This time, unlike ten years ago, Cole had a condom in the pocket of his jeans. Lizzie breathed a sigh of relief that he had remembered protection because, she was embarrassed to admit, she hadn't even considered it. It seemed her brain had stopped working once their clothes had come off.

Lizzie had had teenage dreams of making love to Cole, and adult dreams, but the reality was so much better than either.

Murmuring softly in her ear, he slipped slowly into her with a visible shudder. "Ah, Lizzie."

He raised himself over her with two strong arms and watched her face with every stroke. Between each thrust, he said one thing more incredible than the last. "You are so beautiful. I love you. I always have."

She felt her composure crack at the words she'd dreamed of her entire adult life, and tears welled in her eyes.

He shook his head and wiped her cheeks while still loving her, gently, slowly. "Shhh. Don't cry. I love you."

In a voice choked by tears, she said, "Why?"

That stopped him mid-stroke. "Why?"

She nodded. "Is it because of Mikey?"

He shook his head adamantly. "No, Lizzie. I loved you long before Mikey. I'm sorry I never told you back then."

She nodded tearfully. "I've always loved you, too."

He looked overwhelmingly relieved when he said, "Thank god. Does that mean I don't have to stop?" He looked devilish and she laughed and wiped away her tears.

"No. In fact, I wouldn't mind if you went a little faster."

He leaned down and bit her lower lip gently. "Anything you want, my love."

Cole did what she asked and as her second orgasm shook him into one of his own, he held her tighter and rode the waves right along with her.

When both their bodies finally stilled and their breathing had calmed, Cole looked at her with a pained expression on his face. "Lizzie. I still need to know. Why did you break up with me rather than tell me you were pregnant?"

She owed him this at least. "It's true that I didn't want you distracted. You gave up your scholarship; I wasn't going to be responsible for you losing your career, too. But I also knew you, and I knew you would marry me just because of the baby. I couldn't bear the thought of that. I've loved you for as long as I can remember, I couldn't marry you knowing you didn't do it for love, too."

Cole cupped the face of the woman he loved in both of his hands and fought his fear and insecurities. "Marry me now, Lizzie."

"Why?"

Why? She was one infuriating woman, Cole thought. It was a good thing he loved her. "Because I do love you, you silly woman."

"It's not because of Mikey?"

Cole shook his head. "No. Not because of Mikey. It's because I can't live without you. I want you with me every day and in my bed every night, that's why. I want to grow old with you and make more babies with you. Hopefully the next one will look a little bit like you for a change." He smiled at her.

She looked up at him through her tears and laughed. "Do you always talk so much when you make love?"

He glanced down to where they were still joined. "We had a lot of talking to do. You are real good at avoiding conversations you don't want to have. I figured this way you couldn't get away. And you still haven't answered my question. Lizzie Barton, will you marry me?"

Lizzie nodded and smiled, mimicking him. "Yes, Cole Ryan. I will marry you."

Then he heard the whoop of joy out in the hall and Lizzie looked like she wanted to crawl down into the mattress.

"If there is a certain almost ten year old out in the hall who doesn't want to be grounded for the rest of his life, he had better back away from the door right now," Cole yelled over his shoulder, feeling a little red-faced himself.

"Yes, Dad." He heard Mikey's muffled voice from out in the hall.

Cole was speechless with his mouth hanging open as he looked down at Lizzie. She smiled at him. "Wow."

Cole smiled back, his eyes feeling a little misty. "Yeah, wow." He blew out a breath and pulled himself out of her, reaching for the quilt folded on the end of the bed. He covered her with it, then grabbed and pulled on is boxers and jeans. "Tomorrow, I'm getting a lock for that door."

She laughed. "That's probably a good idea, Dad."

He grinned wider. "Go get your calendar, woman. We have a wedding to plan, and then you have classes at the local college to sign up for."

She frowned but he continued, ignoring her. "You have to get that teaching degree you've put off. Then after you graduate, we can get to work on another baby. Tomorrow, I'm going to call the principal at the school. I heard today the high school baseball team is currently without a head coach." He sat again and laid a hand over her belly. He couldn't wait for the day to come when Lizzie told him she was pregnant again, but he would wait until she'd fulfilled her dream. What was another four years? Probably more like three years knowing how smart Lizzie was. He'd already waited ten years for her and Mikey.

He smiled at her. "That plan OK with you?"

She nodded. "It's just fine."

Cole grabbed her hand and brought it to his lips. "Good. Oh, and I almost forgot." He pulled a small square box out of his pocket and handed it to her.

With trembling hands, she opened and stared down at the tiny diamond ring inside.

"It's so small because it's a promise ring. I bought it for you when we were dating. It was only supposed to be until I gave you a real engagement ring, after I'd made it big. I picked it up the day before your letter arrived. I could never bear to part with it, so I've kept it all this time." His chest still felt tight when he remembered that painful day.

Lizzie was shaking so badly she could barely hold the ring box. Cole took her trembling hands in his. "So, you see. I wouldn't have married you just because you were pregnant. I would have married you because I always wanted to."

Tears streamed down her face unchecked. "I wasted ten years we could have been together."

Cole shook his head. "No, Lizzie. I tried to think about it like that and stay angry with you, but the more I considered it, the more I realized something. We were both so young then and life on the road is hard on wives. On the team, I saw a lot of marriages fail. I honestly can't guarantee we would have made it then. But now, I'm sure." Cole gathered her in his arms. "I know we'll be together until we are old and gray and holding our grandchildren in our arms."

She nodded. "Cole?"

"Yeah."

"Next time you ask me the most important question of my life, can you make sure I have some clothes on?"

He laughed. "Sure. I'll get you a bigger ring and I'll make sure you have at least underwear on when I give it to you."

"Oh, no you won't!"

He shrugged. "OK, naked it is then."

"No, I mean you will not get me a bigger ring." She took what he considered an embarrassingly small diamond out of the box and slipped it on with shaky hands. "This one is perfect."

He smiled and kissed her hand just above the ring. "We'll see. But I do know one thing, you have made my life perfect."

"We'll see how perfect you think life is when you move in here and have to wait on line for the bathroom."

Cole frowned. "Aren't we going to move out once we're married?"

Lizzie shook her head. "I'll only move if it's walking or biking distance from here. I want Mikey to be able to see his grandparents and uncle anytime he wants."

Cole pursed his lips, acting as if he was really considering whether or not that would be all right. Secretly, he'd already looked into buying the empty lot behind the Barton house. He'd find an architect and a builder and hopefully they could be moved in by Christmas.

He finally smiled at Lizzie. "I think that will be OK. I'll see what I can do."

She looked relieved. "Really?"

He nodded. "Really. On one condition."

Lizzie looked skeptically cautious. "What's that?"

"In spite of what just happened here in your parents' house, and the fact that we already have a child together, I do have too much respect for your family to move in here with you until after we're married."

She nodded. "OK. So when are you thinking?"

"I guess tomorrow is too soon. How about next week?"

"Next week?"

He squeezed her hand in his. "Please, Lizzie. I've waited too long already."

She rolled her eyes. "Are you going to throw guilt at me every time you want something?"

"I don't know. Is it working?"

She scowled and made him wait before saying, "OK. Next week it is, but not because of your guilt trip, but because I want to."

He smiled. "Good. Now we better get dressed and get out there. I can only imagine what Mikey is telling everybody."

Lizzie shook her head. "Exactly twice I've had sex with you, Cole Ryan. The first time I got pregnant. The second time I got caught by my son. What's next?"

Cole winked and scooped her into his arms. "That's the beauty of making love with me, sweetie pie. It's just one surprise after the next."

Lizzie ran her hands over his still bare chest. "At least I won't get bored."

"No, my darlin' wife-to-be, you surely won't."

He captured both of her hands and kissed them, and then vaulted off the bed. More touching like that and he'd been in no shape to go out and face the family. "Come on. Get dressed."

"Why? Am I too tempting naked." She let the quilt slip down to her waist.

He swallowed. "Let's see if we can move that date up to tomorrow."

He heard her laughing at him all the way down the hall.

Epilogue

It wasn't the next day, but at least it was the next week, when Cole stood beside Lizzie and said his wedding vows. Bobby and Mikey were his two best men. Lizzie's sister, Mary Sue, had flown home and stood beside her. Both his and Lizzie's parents filled the front church pew. Most of the people filling the remaining seats had known them both since they'd been born.

Cole glanced around at his new family and realized that he, the only child of a service station owner from Pigeon Hollow, had done pretty well for himself to be surrounded by so many people who cared about him.

Bobby winked at him when it came time to hand him the wedding band. Cole noticed his own hands shake as he took the diamond-encrusted circle from him. That had been the compromise. Lizzie could wear the tiny promise ring on her right hand, but her wedding band was going to be something worthy of her. Although no amount of diamonds would be enough to thank her for the son she'd given him.

On the way out of the church, with his wife's hand on his arm, Cole spotted the ever-present television producer and cameramen belonging to Bobby, but there was no camera. Cole didn't even want to think what Bobby had to do to keep the cameras out of the church for their wedding. He'd have to thank him later.

But right now he had something more important to do. He pulled Lizzie by the hand when they reached the sidewalk. "Come on."

"Where are we going? The reception is in the church hall."

"I know. We'll be back, eventually." He pulled her to the car and once he'd tucked her and her white dress safely into the convertible, sped for home.

"Are you dragging me home to have sex?"

"No. Well, not only to have sex. There's something I have to show you."

She looked skeptical, until he pulled up the street behind her parents' house, parked and turned off the car.

"Why are we here?"

"See that big hole in the ground filled with cement?" He went around to her side and pulled her out of the car.

"Yeah."

Scooping her up, he walked across the red clay dirt of the construction site and stepped up onto the poured concrete slab. Then he spun her around as she clutched the ring of fresh flowers that sat on the dark ringlets pinned up on top of her head. "I have just carried you across the threshold of our new home, Mrs. Ryan. What do you think?"

"This is ours?"

"Yup. Bought, paid for and almost built."

She squeezed his neck and smacked quite a kiss on his lips. "I think, that if you don't take me to a house with actual walls really soon, we're going to be giving our new neighbors quite a show."

Cole's heart clenched with love as he grinned and started the walk back to the car. "Mrs. Ryan, I think I am really going to like being married to you."

The End

THE DEPUTY

Chapter 1

Bobby Barton sat in the furthest corner table in the diner, back to the wall so he could watch the door, his friend Jared opposite him. It was a sad day when a man, an officer of the law no less, had to sneak out of his house in the middle of the night just to have a moment of private conversation with a buddy.

While absently playing with the sugar packets on the table, he laid out his plan. "So tomorrow, five-thirty a.m., I'm headin' to the lake to go fishin'. She wants to be with me every wakin' moment? I'll show her exactly how awake I can be! You wanna come?"

Jared winced. "Not really, but I will. You sure are goin' to a lot of trouble to make this girl's life miserable. What'd she ever do to you?"

"You mean besides her and her cameraman tryin' to follow me every damn place I go, includin' inside the stall in the men's room?"

Jared laughed.

"Sure. It's real amusin' for you, Jared. *Your* producer is your girlfriend."

"Yeah, which means I can't let anyone know she's my girlfriend so she doesn't get fired."

Bobby sighed. "All right. So we'll agree this damn show has put a kink in both our lives?"

Jared nodded. "Damn straight. But it's only for eight weeks and it's good for the business 'round here."

Bobby knew Jared was right. Mac had even added an extra shift at the diner when he started staying open 'til the wee hours of the morning to accommodate the television crews who were taping late.

It turned out the local honky-tonk bar in town was providing quite a bit of grist for the television mill. There was a crew at the bar until closing every night. That was why Bobby was safely camera-free at the diner at the moment; the camera crew was still at the bar, hoping to capture drunks at their worst.

His own personal hell—uh, crew—had gone back to their rooms at The Hideaway for the night, thinking he was tucked safely away, asleep in his bed at home.

"She is cute, though." Jared's voice cut into his ponderings about why they'd ever agreed to the taping of this damn reality TV show.

He glanced up at his friend. "Who? Your girlfriend, Mandy? I should hope you think she's cute, you're sleepin' with her."

Jared rolled his eyes. "I was talkin' about your producer, Christy. Don't seem like such a hardship, havin' that pretty face shinin' up at you day and night."

Bobby groaned. Yeah. She was cute. She was also as tenacious as a pit bull and had the nose of a bloodhound. "Maybe under other circumstances I'd agree with you. But damn it, Jared, do you know what I had to do to wrestle that tape of me punchin' Cole away from her?"

Jared grinned. "You still have it? I'd love to watch that. Mr. Cool losin' his head."

Bobby scowled at his supposed friend.

Jared shook his head at him, still grinning. "Oh, stop givin' me that look, Bobby. It's funny. All right. Tell me, what'd you have to do to get the tape? Was it good?" Jared waggled his eyebrows at Bobby.

Bobby sighed and ignored Jared's insinuations in favor of more bitching. "I had to agree to let them ride with me from now on during my shifts. I'd been able to at least get away from them when I was in the patrol car answerin' calls around town. I'd convinced them it was the sheriff's policy, no civilians in the car. But now that's over."

"Hmm. A tape of you punchin' out the famous Cole Ryan at a little league game, or you sittin' in your car drinkin' coffee while takin' a radio call that old Mrs. Brown's cat's stuck in a tree again." Jared made a weighing motion with his hands and cocked a brow. "I don't know. Is that producer of yours not the sharpest tool in the shed?"

Bobby shook his head and shrugged. "All I know is, I would have promised them anything they wanted to get that tape. I couldn't let Lizzie and Mikey go through that kind of embarrassment. *That* whole situation has been strange enough as it is."

Jared blew out a breath. "Tell me about it. Who the hell would have guessed Cole was Mikey's father? You know, there was a time that I was afraid it might be Jack. I actually counted the months from the last time he was home on leave."

"Believe me, I did the same thing. But if it had been Jack, I needn't have worried about killin' him myself, Mary Sue would have done it for me."

Jared laughed. "Got that right. She considered him her property back then."

"When I first found out Lizzie was pregnant, I'd even considered it could be you. Just for a few days, until I figured out it was Cole," Bobby confessed to Jared.

Jared slammed his coffee mug down onto the table. "You knew it was Cole all this time? Ten years?"

Bobby nodded and got very interested in drinking from his own mug.

Jared raised a brow and shook his head. "Well, I guess I know who to go to next time I need a secret kept. You're a friggin' vault."

He shrugged. "Hey, she's my sister. I needed to protect her."

"Sheesh, Cole's lucky you didn't drive out and kill him right there on the pitcher's mound the minute you knew."

"There were times I almost did. In hindsight, it's damn good I didn't, especially now he's my brother-in-law. I never imagined Lizzie was keepin' Mikey a secret from him."

Jared shook his head in agreement. "Women."

Bobby laughed bitterly. "Yup. Can't live with 'em…"

Jared finished the sentiment. "…can't get laid without 'em."

Choking on a swallow of coffee, Bobby laughed. "*Not*

what I was goin' to say, but yeah, that, too."

~

Christy Dunne sat in her boss's room at The Hideaway Motel, currently on the receiving end of a ranting fit being thrown by said boss.

Mandy, her boss and the show's head producer, stormed around the room while yelling.

"You gave up the most valuable tape we've gotten so far! And for what? So you can ride around with Deputy Bobby? This is Pigeon Hollow, Christy. It's not New York, it's not LA. What do you think you're going to capture by riding around in the deputy sheriff's cruiser in a bumfuck town like this? Huh? Just tell me one thing, what the hell were you thinking?"

There was a time, not very long ago, that Mandy's rant would have sent Christy running away in tears. But since their arrival in Pigeon Hollow for this show, Christy had, much to Mandy's chagrin, seen the softer side of her boss. The fact that Mandy was sneaking around with one of the town's main characters made her often bitchy superior actually seem human. And the fact that Christy had stumbled upon her in the midst of a breakdown over Jared Gordon meant that Christy was the only one on the shoot privy to their illicit romance. That fact had to provide her with some modicum of job security. No?

She sure hoped so, since it was not a smart decision to relinquish to Bobby the tape of him knocking former major league pitcher Cole Ryan right on his famous ballplayer's butt. Next to that, the eventual discovery that she'd given in to Bobby's request to not film Cole's wedding ceremony would seem trivial. At least she hoped so, anyway.

"I honestly think that I can get some really great footage by riding with him, Mandy. It will be hysterical to see how he handles even the mundane situations around town. He's so serious all the time; we can edit it to make him like the straight man in a comedy."

Christy couldn't tell her boss the truth, that she would do

just about anything to spend more time in the company of the dashing deputy. Anything so she could run her fingers through that wavy black hair while gazing into those ice blue eyes. Anything to divest him of those khaki uniform pants and wake up with his black cowboy boots parked under her bed.

No, she definitely couldn't tell Mandy all that, even if she had spotted the Gordon truck pulling away from Mandy's room obscenely late at night on more than one occasion.

Mandy stood in front of her now, hands on her hips. "I sure hope you're right, because I've staked my career on this show. If it fails…"

Christy knew what would happen if it failed. They'd both be on line at the unemployment office. The television business in LA was cutthroat, and producers were a dime a dozen. "I can do this, Mandy. I promise, I'm putting my job on the line, too."

Mandy raised her brow. "Yes, you are." Glancing at her watch, she continued. "Why are you back so early?"

Early! Ha! It was midnight now and Bobby was going fishing at the crack of dawn the next day. Maybe losing this job wouldn't be the worst thing in the world.

"Bobby's off work for the night and went to bed already. I waited in the car until after his bedroom light went off just to make sure." And drooled imagining him undressed and slipping under the sheets.

Mmm, mmm. What was she going to tell Mandy again? Oh, yeah. "He—I mean *we*—are going fishing early in the morning."

That actually made Mandy laugh, which didn't happen all that often, as far as Christy knew. "What exactly does a person wear to go fishing?"

"Got me. I guess I'll wear shorts and flip flops in case I have to wade into the water for something." Christy shrugged. Thank goodness the entire crew had been given permission to abandon any semblance of a dress code, given both the heat and the fact that none of them were ever on camera themselves.

Still looking amused, Mandy said, "Better you than me."

"Actually, Bobby said he's inviting Jared to go." Which meant that Mandy and her cameraman, assigned conveniently to Jared for the shoot, should be there, too, theoretically.

As if reading her mind, Mandy raised one perfectly plucked eyebrow. "You don't need two camera crews to go fishing. I'll take my cameraman into town. Maybe Cole Ryan will piss somebody else off enough to take a swing at him."

Christy physically felt that not so subtle verbal slap. Then Mandy continued with a thinly veiled warning. "You just make sure you stick to Deputy Bobby like glue. I mean that."

Oh, Christy had every intention of doing that, direct decree from the boss or not.

Chapter 2

The sun was just making its presence known in the eastern sky when Christy and her cameraman, John Fletcher—Fletch for short—pulled up and parked on the road in front of the Barton house.

Christy spared a moment to take a second glance at the peachy glow on the horizon. She didn't see the sun rise in LA often. There was that one night her girlfriends took her out for her birthday and then to a diner for breakfast after the dance club closed. But she didn't remember noticing the sunrise, no surprise there.

Fletch yawned. "You have no mercy. Dragging a man out to work before his first cup of coffee." The video camera balanced tenuously on his shoulder, making Christy want to put her hand up to steady it.

She put one finger to her lips. "Shhh. I want to sneak in and get him as he's waking up."

Fletch managed to raise a sleepy but suggestive-looking eyebrow. "You're just hoping he's naked."

Christy frowned at him and opened the back door stealthily, hoping he didn't notice she hadn't denied the accusation. It still amazed her how everyone around Pigeon Hollow left their doors unlocked.

Once Mrs. Barton had assured her she was welcome to let herself in at anytime, day or night, she had begun to plan how to best capture Bobby without his being on guard because of the camera. And today's little fishing excursion was the perfect excuse to sneak in and find the man right where she wanted him, in more ways than one, in bed. Which was why she was sneaking in just after five, rather than the five-thirty he'd told her to arrive.

She crept through the silent kitchen and down the hall to where she knew Bobby's bedroom was. Mrs. Barton, the quintessential southern hostess, had given her a tour of the house on the first day. Bobby had scowled the entire time.

At first, Christy had assumed Bobby's reaction to her

being privy to his home-life was caused by embarrassment. He had to be thirty, at least, and he still lived with his parents, in spite of having what appeared to be a good job. That was before Christy gleaned the real situation. Bobby was there to help raise his sister's fatherless son, or *formerly* fatherless son. But that was a whole other story, one that she no longer had possession of the video tape for.

When she had realized that the reason Bobby wanted that tape was because he didn't want his nephew or his sister exposed to the entire world, and not to protect his own reputation, she'd finally given it up to him. But the side bonus, which made up for the reaming she took from Mandy over it, was that he now owed her. For that and for not filming the wedding and she intended to collect.

Her heart started to beat a little faster as she reached Bobby's closed bedroom door. She turned the knob tentatively, not knowing if this was the one door in Pigeon Hollow that would actually be locked.

It turned in her hand and her heart pounded harder as she stepped into the room lit by only the soft glow of early morning light creeping through the half-raised blinds.

He slept with the windows open, a fan propped in one, blowing on him in the bed. It figured he didn't have an air conditioner in his room, even in the summer. He just wasn't the type. Mr. Tough Guy.

He slept face up, on top of the sheets, totally exposed and clad in only colored boxer briefs. In the dimly lit room, Christy's eyes widened. There was a lot of man contained in those briefs. She swallowed and was very aware that Fletch had begun taping next to her.

She glanced back to the underwear, and the man within them. Privately, she'd been torn as to whether this staunch public servant would be a boxer or a brief man. This morning had answered her question. His garment was neither and both at the same time, much like the man himself. Yes, Deputy Bobby—as Mandy called him—was a paradox, all right.

Bobby stirred in his sleep and reached a hand down to scratch himself you-know-where, before rolling over onto his stomach and showing her his other asset. That side was just as nice to look at as the other. This man was definitely a two-sided coin, and both sides were equally attractive.

And then the red glowing numbers on bedside alarm clock read 5:15 and a deafening beeping filled the room. Christy jumped. Fletch cursed. And Bobby, slapping the button, rolled over and made Christy fear for her life, no exaggeration, since it seemed the deputy slept with his weapon right next to his bed.

Gun drawn and wearing a glare that could kill without bullets, Bobby growled, "This here is a good way to get your selves shot." Then, without any sign of self-consciousness, he rose, grabbed a pair of jeans off the bedside chair, and strode into the hall and, she assumed, to the bathroom.

She let out a breath she hadn't realized she'd been holding. "You get all that, Fletch."

"Nearly shit my pants when he pulled that gun, but yeah, I got it."

"Good. Let's give the deputy some privacy and wait in the kitchen." Before he does shoot us, she added silently. Besides, she smelled coffee.

And sure enough, when they reached the kitchen, the light on the coffee maker was on and it was happily dripping away. They may be in Nowheresville, but at least the Bartons had an automatic coffeepot with a timer and Bobby—it had to be him, Mr. Detail—had remembered to set it.

Bobby in his underwear and coffee—life, she decided, was good. She went to the pantry and grabbed three mugs from the cabinet Mrs. Barton had previously showed her and poured them all a cup. Then she sat and waited for Bobby to come in and chew her out.

Feeling much like a bad child trying to get an adult to notice them, she realized that any attention she received from Bobby, even of the negative variety, was good enough. She took a long sip of hot coffee and wondered exactly what that said about her.

~

Bobby was still pissed as hell when they reached his favorite fishing spot and found Jared waiting there, laid out on a log, eyes closed beneath his straw hat. Feeling particularly mean at the moment, Bobby poked him with the toe of his boot on his way past.

"Ow! What the hell you do that for?" Jared sat up and frowned at him.

Bobby hooked a thumb in Christy's direction and, even though he knew she didn't like to talk while the cameras were rolling, said simply, "Ask her."

He watched her press her lips together and shake her head. She was pissed because they'd have to edit that out. Too friggin' bad. Sneaking into a man's bedroom while he's sleeping and defenseless. Well, OK, he did have his gun, but he was in his underwear for god's sake! Not to mention sporting one hell of a morning woody. Christ, they wouldn't broadcast that on television, would they?

Then again, this show was for one of those hundred cable stations he rarely had time to watch, so who the hell knew what they could show. Just great! His cock, flying out to millions of paying subscribers. Not to mention that Christy had stood there ogling him in his underwear for god knew how long. He didn't know which bothered him more.

Why didn't there seem to be any male producers on this crew, only females? A male would never have snuck in and filmed another man waking up in his underwear. They would have known better. He shook his head and cast his line out into the lake, determined to ignore the annoying woman and her cameraman if it killed him.

Jared stood beside him, yawing and casting his own line. "You ready to tell me what's wrong yet?"

"Nope."

Jared shrugged. "All right." Then he yawned again.

Bobby took the time to finally look at him. "You look

like crap. Didn't you sleep last night? You know, if you were up all night with one of the horses, you could have just called and canceled."

Jared got an evil grin on his face. "Oh, a little filly kept me up all night, but it wasn't one of my horses."

Bobby let out a loud breath, even more pissed off now. Jared was managing to get himself laid practically every night, and Bobby was destined to live like a monk for the five or so remaining weeks of filming because of his two shadows back there. Didn't that just figure.

Between Jared's exhaustion and Bobby's anger, there was pretty much silence for most of the morning. Good, he couldn't think of better revenge on Miss Nosy than a few boring hours of tape of two men fishing. The only problem was, it gave Bobby too much time to think.

He began to think back to the last time he'd enjoyed the pleasure of a woman, and he was having trouble remembering. Between trying to set a good example when it came to females for Mikey and working crazy hours for the sheriff's department, his social life was pretty much out to pasture.

And now with the camera up his butt—literally, this morning—there was no hope for rectifying the situation for over a month. No friggin' way was he letting cameras catch him even talking to a woman so they could broadcast it all over television.

The more he thought about it, the more he realized he was afraid to even 'handle' things himself, so to speak, in that department. She probably had the bathroom and his bedroom bugged with microphones or hidden cameras. In fact, the minute he got home, he was going to check. That thought made him even angrier.

These were sad times indeed, when a man couldn't even jerk off in private. He shook his head to himself and cast his line.

Christy watched Bobby and his fishing pole from a safe distance. He was still angry. The man's body language was practically screaming. Between the total silence, even with Jared there, and the continued huffing and head shaking, she was sure he was still steaming about that morning.

Christy huffed out a breath herself. Maybe she had gone over the line. And now she was paying for it with hours of the most boring video she'd ever seen shot. Fletch had even set up his tripod, left the camera running, and laid out under a tree to sleep.

She'd salvage the tape, not that she had any choice in the matter if she wanted to keep her job. She would make the footage funny and the viewers would love it. Cut down in editing, with the minutes, no hours, ticked off on a clock graphic in the corner and some sound effects and music laid in, it would be hysterical to the city viewers who couldn't imagine the attraction of fishing anyway.

But it wasn't worrying about the footage that was bothering Christy most, it was the fact that Bobby was really and truly angry with her. The only guy she'd been interested in for what seemed like forever, and she had no hope with him. First, he was off-limits because he was in the show. Not that it mattered, because he hated her anyway. And her efforts to throw them together more by bargaining to be allowed to ride in his patrol car had just gotten him madder.

She sucked when it came to men. And when she glanced at her watch and noted that they were coming up on their third hour of silent, fishless fishing, she realized she sucked at being an assistant television producer, too.

Chapter 3

Bobby glanced at his watch and reeled in his line. He slapped Jared on the back and turned to go. "Time for work."

Jared, half asleep on his feet, jumped. "Already? But I was having so much fun." He reeled up his line, too.

"What're you doing for the rest of the day?" Bobby asked his sarcastic friend.

"I'm thinkin' I need to inventory the hay bales."

Bobby laughed at Jared's code for hiding in the hay room to take a nap. He glanced up and saw Christy already on her cell phone. "I'm thinkin' my jailor is already on the phone to yours and you better run and hide quick before the camera finds you."

Jared squinted in Christy's direction in the morning sunlight. "Hmm. Good thing I know a short cut."

Bobby smiled. "Good thing. See ya later."

"Yup. Have fun."

Watching him sprint for his truck like a racehorse out of the starting gate, Bobby wondered why he couldn't treat this whole thing like a game the way Jared did. Then again, Jared always viewed life as a game. He guessed it was hard not to when your life revolved around watching horses fuck...

"Where to now?" Christy interrupted his thought. Yup, he couldn't even *think* the word and she was there. Forget about actually trying to find a woman to do it with. Nope, not with her around.

He looked his nemesis up and down. It was going to be a hot, humid day, and he could tell this air-conditioning bred girl was already feeling the heat. She'd tied her shirt up around her ribcage, exposing a good amount of stomach between the shirt and her low-rise shorts.

Bobby frowned at himself for even looking.

"Look. I'm sorry. OK? I was wrong. Dead wrong and I will never enter your bedroom again without permission. So can you stop frowning at me so we can move on? If not, the remainder of this shoot is going to be a long five weeks."

She stood directly in front of him, hands fisted on those nicely rounded hips. He raised his eyes from her hips, skimming as quickly as he could past the good amount of cleavage exposed by the low neckline of the shirt and tried to concentrate on her face as she glared up at him with her piercing green eyes.

He nodded once. "Fine."

"Fine what?"

"I accept your apology. Now I've got to get home, change and get to work." He started for the car when he heard tiny footsteps running to catch up with him. He paused and gave her time to run around in front of him again.

"Wait. You promised we could ride with you."

She was worried he'd back out of their deal. He could see it on her face. "So, come on then. I said you could ride with me, I didn't say you could make me late for work."

He continued walking toward the car and smiled at the sounds of the harried scuffle to break down the equipment behind him. He'd forgive her, and he'd follow through, good to his word, and let them ride with him, but he'd be damned if he'd make it easy for them.

~

Christy sat in the corner of the sheriff's office and watched Bobby. It was a lot like watching paint dry. Sure, he was gorgeous and even observing him doing nothing could be a mouthwatering experience, but it lost some charm knowing that if something, anything, didn't happen soon, her job was toast.

He leaned way back in his chair, booted feet up on his desk, as he read the local newspaper. And that was all, for the past hour and a half. Pigeon Hollow was not a hotbed of crime, to say the least. Maybe she could ask him for the Help Wanted section. She had a feeling if things didn't pick up soon, she'd need it.

Christy glanced at Fletch and caught his eye. He shrugged at her, and then continued to work on his crossword puzzle, the video camera back on the tripod for the second time that day.

She sighed, not for the first time during this eternal sit-around-and-wait game she was playing. It was almost as if...no, he wouldn't...would he?

"Did you somehow arrange for there to be no calls today?" She stood, hands on her hips, and accused him.

He lowered the paper slowly and raised a brow. "Would I do that?" he shot back, his tone saying to her he might just do exactly that.

She felt her mouth fall open. "Bobby!" She dropped back down into her chair and buried her face in her hands. Breathing heavily, she tried to calm her panic.

She was so screwed.

"What's her problem?" She heard Bobby ask Fletch.

"She's just going to lose her job because she gave up that Cole Ryan tape, that's all."

Christy winced at hearing that. Fletch was trying to help, but she did not want Bobby to know that little piece of information.

She felt a hand on her shoulder and glanced up, realizing Bobby had crossed the room and was standing next to her. "That true?"

He was so tall and strong and stern looking, he'd be frightening if she wasn't already in lust with him.

She looked up at him and shrugged. What could she say? "If I don't come up with something entertaining to replace it, yeah."

Shaking his head, he looked concerned. "I didn't re-route the calls. It's just a slow day." He squatted down and took one of her hands in both of his. Her heart knocked against her ribcage. "But even so, this is Pigeon Hollow. Not much goes on here."

Trying not to pass out from even that small physical contact, she nodded. "I know." And why did she suddenly not care if she lost a thousand jobs, as long as he kept touching her?

His head dropped briefly and she was staring at his

crown of dark curls, and then he looked back up to capture her in that entrancing blue gaze. "If it really means your job, I'll give you back the tape."

Her lips trembled. He was too good to be true, hot *and* nice. Guys like this only existed in romance novels, definitely not in real life, at least not in *her* real life.

She shook her head in answer to his magnanimous offer. "No. Ryan may be a public figure, but I won't expose your nephew like that. Your family deserves some privacy. It'll be all right."

He watched her for a second, as if sizing her up.

Nodding once, he treated her to a crooked grin and squeezed her hand. His form of a thank you. It was more than enough.

And then, thank god, the phone rang.

Bobby smiled. "Let's see what I've got for you." He winked and strode to the phone on his desk. After a few minutes of cryptic one-sided conversation and her not swooning over the fact he'd winked at her, he hung up and looked in their direction.

"Is a swarm of bees settlin' in the rectory entertainin' enough for you?"

She smiled at him. "It'll do."

"Good. Get your stuff together. I have to call the bee wrangler, then we can go." Bobby began flipping through the ring of business cards on his desk. Apparently, he'd had to call the bee wrangler before because his number was in the Rolodex. Once she got over that surreal realization, she started to plan shots and voiceovers in her head.

"You getting this?" she hissed to Fletch.

"Yup."

Small town law enforcement; wrangling bees rather than criminals. Good television, indeed. This day was beginning to look up, after all.

~

"Narrate for the camera, Bobby. Tell the viewer what's happening." Christy instructed him.

Resisting the urge to groan—he so hated talking to the camera lens as if it were a person—he began to explain the situation.

"The pastor's wife called the sheriff's office with an SOS regarding a bee swarm in the rectory. Apparently, they're not sure if the pastor is allergic to bee stings. Understandably, she was in quite a panic. I instructed them to remain outside of the home until both myself and the local bee wrangler could arrive and assess the situation." He kept his eyes on the road and pretended he was delivering a report to the sheriff, not a damn camera, and things went a little easier.

On the phone, the pastor's wife had asked him to hurry. The moment Bobby pulled his patrol car up to the scene, Fletch and his video camera in the front passenger seat still rolling, he knew why. The pastor, dressed in nothing but a towel, was with his wife outside on the front lawn. The pastor looked so scared, he would have been shaking in his boots, had he been wearing any.

From what Bobby could glean from the old couple's ramblings, the bees had settled in the attic. But being that the rectory was an old building, a good number of them had traveled down the walls and out a crack into the bathroom, where the pastor had been getting out of the shower.

He had to give Christy credit, she wasn't laughing at the old man in his tiny towel, but he could tell she was struggling.

"Pastor, why don't you go into a neighbor's house for a bit, until we get the bees cleared out?"

"But..." the old man glanced down at himself. "I need at least my pants."

Bobby sighed. "I'll go in and get you something to wear."

He headed across the lawn and up onto the front porch. The pastor's wife was still calling out instructions to him as he was opening the door, something about where the pastor's pants may be located within the house. He tried his best to listen, even as he saw Christy covering her mouth with her hand to keep from laughing. Bobby finally gave up waiting for the eternal instructions to be completed and told the woman he would find her husband's pants, the ones that fit, not the ones that didn't, and let the door slam shut behind him.

By the time he'd dodged the few poor confused bees stuck in the house, located not only the pants, but also a shirt and slippers, he arrived outside to find the wrangler he'd called pulling up to the curb.

The guy was old as dirt, but he knew his bees, and he'd come running every time Bobby had called him, which was surprisingly often. Old time beekeepers like him made their living selling honey and catching the occasional errant swarm. But Bobby suspected it was the thrill of the hunt and capture that they liked the best. He knew enough not to ask any questions or they would talk your ear off telling bee tales.

"Hey, Harry. From what I can tell, they're in the attic. Looks like they went in the vent. But there's a set of those pull down stairs, so you have access from the second floor." Bobby laid out the situation for the wrangler. He'd been on enough swarm calls that he knew what Harry needed to know.

"Good. Sounds like an easy one. Maybe I'll let the kid handle it solo." Harry tilted his head to indicate *the kid* and for the first time, Bobby noticed some slick young guy, wearing not nearly enough clothing, chatting up Christy off camera.

He frowned. "Who's that? You usually either work alone or bring one of the other guys from the Backyard Beekeepers Association with you."

"I'm gettin' too old to be crawlin' in attics and climbin' up on roofs, Bobby. 'Bout time I started trainin' someone to do the dirty work for me." The old guy pulled his navy ball cap lower on his brow as he spoke.

Bobby continued to watch Christy and the dirt bag—uh,

apprentice wrangler—talking. "Think you better get him movin', Harry. The pastor and his wife are real anxious to get back into the house."

Harry glanced at Christy, his apprentice and then back to Bobby, brow raised. Then he laughed. "Gotcha."

Damn old man was too observant for Bobby's liking. So he didn't like some strange guy bothering Christy. She was his responsibility for the moment and he didn't know this kid from Adam. It was no big deal.

With a scowl, Bobby watched tank-top boy grab the equipment and follow Harry into the house. Serve him right if he got stung, wearing those clothes to wrangle a swarm.

He was still steaming when Christy came up to stand beside him. Fletch had been a brave city boy and followed the wranglers in. "What was the shop vacuum for?"

Oh, cut-off shorts boy hadn't explained that to her? "They vacuum up the bees."

She turned to stare at him. "No!"

Bobby had to laugh at her reaction. "Yup."

"And they don't mind?"

Bobby shrugged. "Don't seem to. Course, I'm not there when they get them out of the vacuum, so I don't know."

She shook her head and stared at the house. "Wow."

Since she was so impressed with the bees, he wished he'd listened closer to all of Harry's lectures so he could dazzle her with more of his bee knowledge. But he'd gone through his entire bee repertoire with the vacuum question.

It wasn't very long at all before Harry and his assistant came out, carrying a closed cardboard box and the vacuum. Bobby noticed a few welts on tank top boy's exposed arms and smiled to himself. The satisfaction was short lived, however, when Christy, grabbing Fletch and his camera, ran over to bee boy and started interviewing him.

By the time Bobby strode over to join them, bee boy was saying, "They'll pretty much follow the queen anywhere."

Christy got an evil look on her face. "Oh, so they're all males then." Was she flirting with this kid?

Boy toy laughed. "You'd think so, but no. All the worker bees are females. They're the ones who rear the young, gather the honey and the pollen, and defend the hive. You really learn to respect females when you understand the workings in a hive." He ran a hand through his long locks of blond hair.

The bastard was definitely flirting with Christy, and men should have short hair, in Bobby's opinion.

The kid was still talking. Why was he still talking? They should be done by now. "Actually, there are a low percentage of males, they're called drones, in the swarm, and their only function is to impregnate a new virgin queen."

Oh, ho! And now he'd found a way to bring up the subject of sex. That figured.

Bobby watched Christy raise an amused and flirtatious brow. "So they are like studs, then."

He watched bee boy smile at his producer, eating up the attention. "Yup, but it's not as satisfying as it sounds. You see, the minute they um…mate with the queen, it rips their uh…man parts off. And then they die."

Was sex boy actually blushing? Humph. Bobby could have talked about bee sex on camera without blushing. Any real man could. Jeez.

Christy opened her eyes wide in horror at what sex boy had just told her. "Oh. Ow."

"Exactly." He laughed down at her. Why was he standing so damn close to her, anyway? She giggled back and Bobby nearly vomited.

He finally couldn't stand it any more and stepped forward. "Can we wrap this up here so I can get back to work?"

Christy turned to him hopefully. "Did another call come in?"

Bobby scowled. "No."

"Then can't we stay? This is great stuff." She looked at him with those pleading 'I'm going to get fired because of you' eyes and he gave in, taking a step back again to observe from afar.

He heard Harry chuckling beside him. "That little girlie givin' you some grief?"

Bobby rolled his eyes. "You don't know the half of it."

Finally, after what seemed like forever, Christy ran back to the car to get two release forms, Harry and pretty boy signed them, and then the three of them were finally back in Bobby's car.

Although Bobby's relief at being rid of bee boy seemed destined to be short lived. In the back seat, he heard Christy shuffling papers as she filed her precious releases, then he heard a "Hmm."

"What?" He glanced at her in the rearview mirror.

"Um, nothing." She looked up at his reflection in the mirror. She was a terrible liar.

"Tell me."

"Really, it's nothing."

"Christy…"

"Fine, it's just that, when Corey signed his release, he, um, wrote something on it."

Corey? Was that the boy toy's name? That figured. Bobby parked in a spot on Main Street and turned in his seat to look at her, face to face. "What exactly did *Corey* write?"

"Um, his phone number, and 'call me' next to it… with a smiley face."

A smiley face? Well, wasn't that just perfect. "And?" Bobby demanded.

"And what?" Christy was staring.

He didn't care, he asked his question anyway. "Are you going to call him?"

She shrugged. "Maybe." Was she being coy? Did he even know what exactly 'being coy' was?

Bobby frowned. *Maybe?* What kind of answer was that?

"Why do you care?" She'd turned the questioning back around on him.

"I care because for better or worse, while you're in this town, you are my responsibility. You don't know anything about that guy."

"I know he works for a friend of yours. Isn't that enough?"

Just because Harry knew bees, didn't convince Bobby he was a fine judge of character when it came to dates for his producer! "No. There are scam artists all over the world."

She rolled her eyes. "Yeah, like a scam artist would pretend to be a bee wrangler in Pigeon Hollow."

Bobby let out a frustrated huff. "You can date whoever you want when you go back to LA, but when you are in Pigeon Hollow, you are mine. You got that?"

Christy's eyes opened wide, causing Bobby to review what he'd just said and decide it hadn't come out exactly the way he'd wanted.

Not knowing quite how to fix the situation, he turned back to face forward and noticed the red light blinking on the camera up on Fletch's shoulder. "What the hell are you doing?"

"My job. And stop talking to me, I'm invisible, remember."

Bobby had no answer for that, so he just scowled and slammed his way out of the car, wondering exactly when he'd lost control of his life.

Chapter 4

Bobby was jealous! She couldn't believe it. She hesitated to let herself believe it, but the proof was there. He'd nearly had a meltdown over Corey giving her his phone number.

She hadn't even seriously entertained calling him. That is, until she saw Bobby's jealousy over even the remote possibility she might. Who knew all it took was a little competition to pique his interest in her. Hmm. Well, now that she had his interest, she better figure out what the hell to do with it.

Christy was just considering if she had any sexy clothing in her suitcase when Bobby had pulled up in front of the diner. She hadn't even noticed it was nearly lunchtime, but her stomach grumbled at just the thought of food. She could definitely eat one of Mac's famous burgers with onion rings about now. That was not a problem.

The problem was finding a place to situate Fletch so he could get a clear shot of Bobby in the packed diner. She finally charmed Mac into letting Fletch stand behind the counter, with the understanding that there was a penalty of death for them both if they got in the waitress' way. Christy felt an instant sympathy for the camera crew that had been assigned to Mac fulltime. That must be a real joy for them.

Christy managed to wolf down her burger, then held the video camera so Fletch could do the same, all within the time it took Bobby to finish his own sandwich, pie and coffee. How did he keep that hard body eating pie at every meal? Jared did it, too. She was convinced that southern men had different metabolisms then the rest of the world. The women, however, were apparently not so blessed, she thought as she watched the chubby waitress refill Bobby's mug.

She frowned as she watched Bobby smile at Misty the waitress and saw the girl blush, all through the viewfinder of the camera. Hmm. Was she a bit jealous herself? She really shouldn't be. Besides the fact that she had no claim on

Bobby, she hadn't seen nor heard a word breathed about him being involved with anyone in town. Or out of town, for that matter. The man apparently lived like a monk, or at least left that public impression. Who knew, maybe he was some wild swinger or internet porn mogul. Yeah, sure! Mr. Morality. Not a chance.

That was probably going to be the bigger challenge, not competing against other women, but battling Bobby's high morals, or perhaps just lack of interest in sex. But how could a man who looked like that not be interested in sex? That would be like having a racecar and leaving it parked in the garage.

Thinking back to the hissy fit Bobby had thrown over the bee wrangler, Corey might possibly be her best bet to get Bobby to finally pull his car out...and park it in her garage. Mouth watering from more than the smell of apple pie baking in Mac's kitchen, she smiled at that thought.

Between her mind racing with thoughts of Bobby and the image of him filling the viewfinder of the camera, she didn't even hear anyone approach her. Not until a familiar voice said, "Hey, beautiful. Fancy seeing you here."

Through the lens, she saw Bobby react as she said, "Hey, Corey. What are you doing here? Don't you have a few thousand angry bees in a vacuum that need releasing somewhere?"

She heard him laugh. "Sure did. We dropped them off at the observation hive over at the kid's nature center. Then Harry asked me to run in and get him something to eat. So...you have a chance to look at that form I signed?"

She was deciding exactly what to say when she realized that things were suddenly happening around her. Fletch grabbed the camera and relieved her of her temporary duty as Bobby stood, looking like he was torn between punching out Corey and just turning and leaving. For an officer of the law, he sure had a temper on him. Better not risk another Cole Ryan incident, although it would make good tape.

She turned to Corey. "I'm kind of busy right now. Can I

talk to you later?" She said it loud enough for Bobby to hear. She hoped she wasn't leading Corey on. But after all, she never promised she would date him, just that she'd talk to him later.

Corey was cute enough, but a bit too much of an aggressive flirt for her taste. She almost laughed thinking that Bobby, on the other hand, wasn't nearly aggressive enough in his attentions to her. At the moment, Christy was feeling very much like Goldilocks. Was there no man who was just right? Did 'just right' even exist outside of fairytales? That was a question for later, because Bobby had made his decision and was halfway to the diner's exit.

"Misty, throw this on my tab. Corey, I gotta go."

He flashed perfect white teeth at her. "You better call me!"

Shaking her head at the fact that it was the wrong man wanting her to call him, she ran to catch up with Bobby before he left her, which it looked like he was about to do.

She flung herself into the back seat and just managed to slam the door shut behind her when he pulled away from the curb. She watched Fletch raise a brow and had to smile. Oh, yeah. She had Bobby right where she wanted him now. Maybe. As long as silent and angry was better than silent and aloof, she definitely was winning him over.

As he drove away from the diner, Bobby's cell phone vibrated in his pocket. He pulled it out while keeping one hand on the wheel. According to the caller ID read out, it was the sheriff. He flipped it open. "What's up?"

"You available?"

"Sure. What've you got?" Bobby prayed it didn't involve bees. He'd had more than enough of bee boy for one day.

"Horse loose out on Leap Frog Road."

"Could it be one of Gordon's?" That wasn't too far from Jared's farm.

"Nope, already called him. He checked. All his are accounted for. He did say if you need any help or a trailer, just call."

Bobby blew out a breath. "Will do." He disconnected the phone and made a u-turn. He was still in just bad enough of a mood over bee boy to withhold where they were going from Christy. It was petty, but it made him feel better. Glancing in the rearview mirror, he could see the suspense was killing her. Good!

He considered the situation, the one with the horse, not the one with Christy and bee boy. He should call Jared for help. It would probably take him and both of his farm hands to catch a spooked loose horse. Although Christy would probably come home with the phone numbers of both of Jared's employees, too. Hmm. Maybe he could handle the horse himself.

"Would you like to tell us where we are going, Deputy?" He guessed she finally couldn't take it any more.

Purposely not elaborating, he stated it as simply as he could. "There's a loose horse over on Leap Frog Road."

He heard Fletch snort softly, whether it was over the loose horse or Leap Frog Road, he didn't know. He didn't get city folks.

"And...? What are you going to do about it?"

She was trying to get him to elaborate for 'the viewers' as she was always saying.

Well, he wasn't in the mood for elaboration at the moment.

"Catch him," he said. It was the truth and it said all he needed to say.

He caught her scowl in the mirror and smirked to himself. She wanted to play around with bee boy? Ha! He'd show her how to play games.

The good news was that by the time they arrived at the scene, it appeared the horse's owner was already there. The bad news was that the horse was good and truly spooked.

Thinking that the last thing the horse needed was his patrol car frightening him more, Bobby parked far away. Before going over to talk to the owner, he set up flares in the

140

road. The other thing the horse didn't need was to get hit by a driver unaware of the danger.

He walked up to the young girl standing in the road looking very flustered. "He yours?"

She nodded. "I don't know how he got out, though."

"We'll figure that out later. Let's just worry about getting him back in for now."

Bobby saw the girl looking over his shoulder and realized his shadows must be back there. He hooked a thumb in their direction. "Ignore them."

She raised a brow and then stared at him, suddenly smiling. "Sure, deputy. Whatever you say." Her eyelashes fluttered.

Great, now she was flirting with him. "You got a bucket of feed and a lead rope?" Bobby suggested, getting them back to the task at hand. She continued to stare at him and nodded but didn't make a move.

Bobby raised a brow. "You wanna go get 'em?"

She smiled wider. "Sure."

Finally turning, she swayed her narrow hips all the way across the road and headed for a barn not too far away.

Bobby shook his head. He didn't even own a horse and he knew better what to do than this girl. He knew the farmer who lived there. He hadn't realized how old his daughter had gotten, though. Hmm. That old man had his hands full with that one, but she wasn't Bobby's problem, although this loose horse sure as hell was.

He glanced back to the horse. It was big. Real big. Looked like a draft horse breed. Guessing it weighed close to a ton, with no exaggeration, he was just considering what damage a ton of scared horse could do when Christy appeared next to him.

"Get back in the car," he said flatly.

She frowned at him, planted her hands on her hips and glared. "No. Why? So you can flirt with the proverbial farmer's daughter in her cut-off shorts that leave her ass cheeks hanging out?"

He raised a brow at Christy. This, he really didn't need right now. And who was she to accuse anyone of flirting? Clenching his jaw, he repeated. "Get back in the car."

"If you want to be mad at me, fine. But you can't stop me from doing my job!"

"And you can't stop me from doin' mine. It's not safe out here. Get back in the car or you'll never ride with me again."

Never one to not argue when given the opportunity she huffed and had just opened her mouth to say something else when the horse decided he didn't like it on that side of the road any longer, and came galloping straight at them.

Thank god Fletch was out of the horse's path, shooting the scene from the side of the road, because Bobby had barely enough time to save himself and Christy. They were both about to be trampled, and she showed no sign of moving. Bobby didn't take the time to think about it, he simply picked her up, flung her over his shoulder and ran. The horse passed them so closely he felt its tail hit his shoulder.

Bobby watched the horse run directly to the girl and the bucket of feed. That had been what spurred the gallop, the damn food.

Since they seemed to be safe, he dumped Christy back on the ground but left his hands around her waist when he felt how unsteady she was. Then he realized his hands were against her warm bare exposed skin. Their eyes met for a moment. Insanity must have overtaken him because he nearly lowered his head toward her mouth.

Then he spotted the red light on the camera and dropped his hands immediately, watching her sway on her feet after he released her. He took one giant step back. "You OK?"

She nodded.

"Good." He nodded back and strode across the road. He needed to check on that horse.

Chapter 5

The rest of the day was uneventful compared to nearly getting trampled, and Christy could honestly say that she was never happier to see her bed at The Hideaway. Her only complaint was that morning seemed to come much too soon and was heralded by Mandy pounding on her door at the crack of dawn.

Christy shuffled to the door, flung it open and then crawled back into bed, not bothering to close it behind her guest. She frowned at how awake, not too mention chipper, Mandy appeared at this ungodly hour. Dressed for the day and carrying a clipboard, she looked ready for a board meeting when Christy was barely ready for a shower.

She nearly groaned as a to-go cup of coffee was thrust at her, meaning that Mandy had already been to town and back. Whatever, as long as she brought her coffee, Christy didn't care if she'd been to Mexico and back already.

"So. You have been busy. Fletch dropped off the tapes from yesterday at my room last night."

Christy did her best to assess whether Mandy was actually pleased, or being sarcastic. It was a tough call, so she simply nodded and waited.

"I have a idea…" Mandy began.

Uh, oh. Mandy's ideas usually meant more work for Christy, but wasn't that always the way? When the boss got a vision, the assistant usually had the dubious pleasure of making it reality.

Mandy continued. "You have the night off tonight."

Christy raised her eyebrow. There was definitely a catch somewhere. "And…"

Mandy smiled. "You know me too well. And you will be going on a date with this Corey character, accompanied by my cameraman."

Christy nearly dropped her precious coffee at that. "Wha…but…huh?"

Mandy plopped her business-casual designer-clad butt

on the edge of the mattress. "Here's my plan. While you are on your date with the studly bee wrangler, I've arranged for a guys' night out over at Jared's. He's inviting Bobby and a few others from town. Fletch will go solo to tape that. I'm guessing the men will speak more freely in a room with no women present and Fletch is good at blending into the background."

Christy did feel a bit silly complaining about a night off after the crazy hours she'd been putting in lately, but she really didn't want to go on a date with Corey. She told Mandy exactly that.

That earned her a sigh in response. "Look, it is obvious that you and Bobby are hot for each other."

That opened Christy's eyes, even more than the strong coffee had.

Mandy laughed. "No use denying it. The chemistry between you two is practically palpable on tape. The way he saved you from that big horse yesterday and when he gets angry just seeing you speaking to that wrangler...Whew, women will be fanning themselves all over the country. It's great TV. Like it or not, you are now one of the characters on *Smalltown, USA*, the next big reality show to hit the small screen."

Christy's mouth dropped open. "But, isn't crew fraternizing with the townspeople against the rules?"

"Sometimes the rules have to change. Especially when *someone* gives away our best piece of tape and we have to come up with another angle for one of the town's main characters." Mandy raised a brow pointedly.

Was she never going to let Christy live down that Cole Ryan incident? This was blackmail, no doubt about it.

"So if you want to play up the angle with me and Bobby, why am I going on a date with Corey?"

Mandy frowned at her. "The date is to make Bobby jealous, of course. You really have no clue about men, do you?"

Christy scowled. "I do, too."

144

Mandy wasn't so smart; Christy had thought of making Bobby jealous over Corey herself. She just hadn't planned on actually going on the date to do it.

"When was your last serious boyfriend? No, forget that. When was your last casual date, even?"

When Christy couldn't come up with one in recent memory, Mandy cried, "Exactly! Trust me on this one. I'll have you and Bobby rolling in the hay before the week is out."

Rolling in the hay? Christy was sure that phrase had never left Mandy's mouth before her association with Jared. Gordon Equine did have that giant hay room. Christy had a gruesome vision of her boss rolling around naked in it and cringed. Too much information.

She sighed. Back to the problem at hand. "All right. I'll go, but no cameras on my date."

Mandy smiled. "I guess I can live with that."

Being forced by your boss to date one hot guy just to win the heart, or at least another piece of anatomy, of another. Christy sighed again. Love in the new millennium. Hmm, good title for a new show. She'd have to remember to write that down.

~

Bobby sat in the kitchen of his parents' house sipping the day's first cup of coffee when his cell phone vibrated in his pocket. Early for calls, he thought, especially when he saw it was Jared. Shouldn't he be shoveling manure or something about now?

"What's got you on the phone so early this morning?" Bobby generally dispensed with small talk as a rule.

"You got tonight off from work?"

"Yup. Why?"

"Poker game, my place, around eight." Jared wasn't much for small talk today either.

Bobby frowned. "We haven't played poker in years. What brought this on?"

"I've been watching those Texas Hold 'Em competitions

145

on TV."

"We always played Five Card Stud."

"So we'll try something different. Just have your butt over here tonight and stop arguing."

Bobby breathed in and out slowly. "All right."

"Oh, and bring some beer."

Shaking his head, he asked, "Anything else?"

"Nope, that's it. See ya." Then Bobby heard a click as Jared hung up.

Bobby was just considering Jared's strange new poker obsession when Christy and Fletch appeared at the back door. "Got something you might enjoy for tonight. Jared is holding a poker game."

Christy's cheeks turned pink and her eyes dropped to the floor briefly. "Good. But you'll only have Fletch tonight. Mandy gave me the night off."

He frowned at her. "You never take time off."

She shrugged. "Mandy insisted."

Hmm. "Good for you. She works you too hard."

Christy colored deeper, leaving Bobby wondering if perhaps there was some female issue he wasn't aware of. And if Christy's embarrassment involved PMS or cramps or something like that, it was best to just let the whole subject drop.

He took one last swallow of coffee and stood. "Ready for another day at the sheriff's department?"

Christy nodded. She was much quieter than usual. Must be PMS. He nodded back at her. "Good, let's try not to get ourselves killed in a stampede today, shall we?" And with that, they were out the door for another day of Pigeon Hollow law enforcement.

Bobby was happy that the day contained no wild bee swarms, no loose draft horses and thankfully, not as much heat and humidity as the last week had. He was not so happy that Jared's prediction did come true and Mrs. Brown's cat got stuck up a tree—again—and Bobby had to climb up and get him. He was beginning to think the cat did it just for the attention.

At least Christy seemed to enjoy seeing him perched up on a limb getting scratched by the damn feline. If it saved her from getting fired and he could keep the infamous little league tape, he guessed it was all worth it. Anything for the sake of the show.

He'd gotten Cole to coach Mikey's game that day. That would keep the cameras away from his family as much as possible. Otherwise, the day was basically uneventful. Christy left him with Fletch that evening, leaving him to eat dinner alone at the diner. Picking up two six-packs of beer for Jared's little gathering, he headed over to the farm thinking that, if nothing else, at least he wouldn't be home watching television and bored.

Nope, *bored* was not a word for that evening, but *strange* sure was. That he discovered when he let himself in Jared's back door and found the strangest mix of poker players he could have imagined. Mac the middle-aged diner owner, Harry the ancient bee wrangler, Jared the horseman and himself the deputy. Oh, and Fletch the big city cameramen. And then it hit him. Mandy must have staged this for the show because these four particular people had never before even thought about getting together to play poker in Jared's mama's kitchen.

Bobby shook his head, shoved one six-pack in the fridge and took his seat with the other, mentally trying to calculate when the hell this show would be over. Tomorrow, he was going to start a countdown on his calendar. That would make him feel better. Although his stomach fell a bit at the thought of never seeing Christy again after spending day and night with her for weeks. That didn't mean anything, though. He'd just gotten used to her, that was all.

Four beer caps popped off, and then Jared started to deal the cards. "Let the games begin, boys. No limit Texas Hold 'Em, and stop rolling your eyes at me, Bobby. I'm not blind."

Bobby smiled and took a sip of his beer. Jared sure was

blind, blinded by love that is if he let Mandy talk him into this. But he didn't say that out loud, since the camera was there. He did however, offer a silent thank you to whoever controlled such things that he himself had never been, and hopefully never would be, likewise afflicted with the love bug.

The cards dealt, Bobby glanced at his and found a pair of twos. Not bad, he'd stick with that.

Harry peeked at his own cards and shoved them into the middle of the table. "I fold. So, Bobby, that cute little brunette you were with yesterday is out with my wrangler tonight."

Bobby nearly dropped his bottle. "Excuse me?"

"Yeah. What's her name? Chrissy?"

"Christy," Bobby corrected through clenched teeth.

"Yup. That's the one."

Bobby glanced around the strange group. Mac looked mildly interested, Jared was totally engrossed in staring at the two cards in his hand and Fletch seemed to be biting his lip. He turned back to Harry. "Where'd they go, you know?" Bobby was doing his best to sound casual.

Harry shrugged. "Nope. But knowing Corey, she'll be back as his place by tonight. That kid's real popular with the ladies."

Bobby realized he was gripping his longneck bottle so tightly his knuckles were white. He put the bottle down and stared at it as the game continued around him.

Why would Christy go out with bee boy? Why didn't she mention it today when she told him she had the night off? And most importantly, why was he suddenly feeling ill?

His concentration was totally shot for the night. He managed to lose his entire twenty-buck buy-in by the end, which was hard to do since each poker chip was worth only a dime.

But it wasn't losing his money that had him worried. It was the sick feeling in his stomach at the thought of Christy with the supposed ladies' man that had him most concerned.

Chapter 6

Christy stood on the chair and looked at her reflection in the mirror over the bureau in her room. Would it kill the owners of The Hideaway to put a damn full-length mirror in the room? Jeez.

She gingerly crawled off the chair and was happy to be safely on the floor in her high-heeled sandals. The flirty little sundress she was wearing looked cute, but she would have rather been wearing it for Bobby. She swiped on some lipstick, threw the tube, along with her room key and a twenty-dollar bill into her date purse and was ready. Now all she needed was her date.

There was a knock on the door and she sighed; be careful what you wish for. She opened the door to Corey's gleaming smile. He leaned down, slapped a big kiss on her cheek, and then walked past her into the room.

She hadn't intended on inviting him in, but it seemed he had other ideas as he threw himself onto her bed. "I've never been inside one of these rooms before. It's not bad."

Easy for him to say, try living there for two months. She didn't say that, however, because knowing Corey, he'd take it as an invitation to move in with her. "Um, are we going to go?"

"Sure. Whatever you want, beautiful." He rose from the bed, hooked an arm around her waist and steered them out the door to a suped-up sports car, complete with tinted windows, spoiler and ear-deafening sound system. She was not one bit surprised.

"I wish you'd let me take you to dinner," Corey commented when they were on the road to the ice cream parlor, her choice after a bit of arguing with him.

"I'm a simple girl. Ice cream is just fine for me." Besides, she did not want to feel any more guilt about going out with him just to make Bobby jealous than she already did. And she definitely did not want to feel like she owed Corey anything if he had paid for her meal. She had a bad feeling it was going to be a battle to keep her virtue intact as it was. He'd already been on her bed, for god's sake! He had ideas about this date, and she was not about to encourage him.

"Well, it's still early. Maybe we can hit the drive-in for a movie after."

She glanced down at the console in between their seats. That might offer some protection from unwanted advances, but she doubted it. Corey seemed like a real problem solver when the motivation was right. Not for the first time that night, and definitely not for the last she was sure, she wished she was with Bobby. This scheme had better work.

"I don't think the movie is a good idea, Corey. I have an early morning tomorrow. Deputy Bobby starts his day about sunrise."

Corey glanced sideways at her. "What's up with Deputy Bobby, anyway? The guy seems pretty possessive when it comes to you."

"Really? You think so?" Her heart beat a little faster at that thought, and she probably sounded more excited than she should have.

Corey glanced back at her again and frowned. "Yeah." He looked back at the road when he asked, "What's going on here, Christy?"

She hung her head for a second debating whether to deny it or tell him the truth. "Look, Corey. You are really cute and I really do like you..."

"Jeez, you're dumping me and we haven't even gotten to our date yet? Why did you even call me?"

She swallowed. "I'm sorry. It was my boss's idea and it sucks and if I had any balls at all I would have told her to take a giant leap." Her shoulders slumped. "It was a shitty thing to do, and I apologize."

Corey pulled up along the curb in front of the ice cream shop and turned in his seat to look at her. Pretty ashamed, she forced herself to look back. Reaching out, he laid one arm along the back of her seat. "Yeah, it was shitty. But I believe it wasn't your fault. So, how about a deal?"

Her eyes narrowed. "What kind of a deal?"

He grinned at her. "There's a girl in town who won't give me the time of day, and that's her car parked right in front of us. You go inside with me, pretend for a little while that I am your dream man and you can't keep your hands off of me, and we'll call it even."

Figuring she owed him at least this much, she agreed, and spent the next hour hanging on Corey in a booth, sharing a triple scoop sundae. Except for the one time when he tried to feed her the cherry with his mouth, he was the perfect gentleman. Being that they attracted the attention of quite a few of the locals, Christy had to wonder if word would get back to Bobby.

Her wondering was over the next morning when she walked into the Barton's kitchen and felt a distinct chill radiating from Bobby's icy glare. She had the definite feeling he knew about her little date, only he didn't know it was pretend.

She was barely inside the room, Fletch on her heels and already filming as if he was expecting some action, when Bobby stood. "You two might as well go back to the motel."

She frowned. "Why?"

"I'm not working today." Somehow, she didn't think that was the real reason. She was re-evaluating her original theory that Bobby was acting cold towards her. He definitely was, but beneath the surface, she could see red-hot anger bubbling.

As if small talk would correct the situation, she said, "So then what are you going to do for the day? Doesn't Mikey have a game or something?"

"I don't want you anywhere near Mikey."

She drew in a quick breath. "Oh." Ouch. That one really hurt. She was having trouble maintaining her composure in the face of his overt antagonism and realized that if she didn't leave and fast, she'd be in tears. She turned and pushed past Fletch and ran out of the door and all the way to

151

the car. If Fletch didn't follow her in the next three seconds, she was leaving him.

Bobby sat back down in the chair and buried his face in his hands. Christy looked like she was about to cry and he felt like the biggest shit south of the Mason-Dixon line. Blowing out a frustrated breath, he lowered his hands and realized that although Christy had fled, Fletch and the camera remained, red light still blinking.

"Why are you still here? Shouldn't you go with your producer?"

"*Associate* producer and no, my job is now to shadow you, with or without her."

Bobby raised his brow. "And why is that?"

Fletch grinned from behind the camera. "Because you are such an interesting guy?"

"Don't fuck with me, Fletch. I'm not in the mood."

"Why *are* you in such a bad mood?" Fletch, who usually never spoke while taping, seemed to be interviewing him. What the hell was going on?

"That's none of your goddamn business." Bobby rose and Fletch took a step back, banging into the screen door behind him.

Smart man.

"It seems you have some issues to work through, so I'm just going to leave you alone for a little while." He lowered the camera from his shoulder and flipped it off. "But I have one thing to say. This is a tough business, man. And I don't mean the long hours and the crap starting pay. I mean it's cut-throat, especially for women who refuse to sleep their way into a job."

"What does any of this have to do with me?"

"Mandy put her job on the line backing this show. Then Christy gave up that probably Emmy winning tape of Ryan to you. We are all scrambling to make this thing work."

Bobby, still feeling mean, said, "You worried about your job, Fletch?"

He shook his head. "Nope. They never fire the technical

152

crew. It's the heads that get chopped when a project fails."

It all came back to that damn tape. "I offered to give her the tape back."

Fletch shook his head. "Christy doesn't want it. She's got morals, which is why it took her twice as long as it should have to land this crap associate producer's job. What I'm trying to say is, don't take it out on Christy. She had nothing to do with any of what's going on."

Bobby squinted at him. "And what is going on?" There was more here than met the eye.

Fletch just shook his head and opened the screen door. "Just remember what I said. Cut her some slack."

Bobby crossed the kitchen in two strides and laid a hand on Fletch's shoulder. "Tell me what's up."

He watched the cameraman breath in and out, looking torn. "You know her pretty well, in spite of the fact that you spent the first few weeks we were here trying to avoid us. If she does anything that seems...out of character, maybe you should ask yourself why."

Then he turned and went, leaving Bobby to wonder again what the hell was going on. He didn't have any clue, and Fletch wasn't offering up anything but riddles, but he bet he knew who might have some answers. Bobby got in his car and headed for Gordon Equine.

No surprise, he found Jared 'taking inventory' in the hay room again. Bobby poked him in the side and Jared woke with a start. "Hey! Quit pokin' me all the time."

"You been burnin' the midnight oil again with Mandy?"

Jared waggled his eyebrows. "More like burnin' the midnight rubber. Ha! Get it? Rubber, as in condoms..."

Bobby held up a hand and groaned. "Yeah. I get it. Thanks for that image." He glanced around. "Hey, how'd you get away from your camera?"

Jared grinned. "Sleeping with the producer has its benefits. Besides, I swore I wouldn't do anything but nap until they got back. How'd you get away from yours?"

"Scared 'em away. I seem to frighten city folk." He

shrugged.

Jared laughed and then rubbed his hands together like a kid whose parents had just left him alone for the first time. "So what do you want to do with our newfound freedom?"

Bobby knew what he wanted, answers. "Does Mandy have something up her sleeve?"

"Um, no?" Jared was a terrible liar.

Bobby raised one eyebrow. "Jared...I know that poker game was staged last night. And now I'm starting to think other things might be as well."

Jared huffed out a breath and sat back down on a bale of hay. "I didn't know what she was planning until after the game last night."

"And what was she planning?"

"She made Christy go on that date last night to stir up trouble for the cameras."

Bobby shook his head, ridiculously relieved and as angry with himself for being mean to Christy as he was at Mandy for thinking up the scheme. "Of all the brainless, idiotic plans..."

"Don't get pissed at her. She's really worried about her job, and ever since Christy gave you that tape..."

"Enough with the fuckin' tape already! One five-minute tape of me punchin' Cole Ryan isn't goin' to make or break this show! And, if you are so all out in love with this girl, I'd think you'd want her to lose her job. You know how far LA is from Pigeon Hollow?"

Jared's face fell. "I know. Don't think I don't consider that every damn day."

"Then let her get fired, marry her and live happily ever after here on the farm."

"I can't."

"Why not?"

"Because I'm scared as hell she'll say no if I ask. And just as scared she'll say yes, hate it here compared to the big city and then end up hating me, too."

Bobby blew out a big breath in sympathy for his friend.

"Love sucks."

"Sure does." Then Jared turned and looked at him closer. "You were pretty distracted last night."

"You insinuatin' something?"

"Maybe. Is there somethin' to be insinuated about?"

Bobby frowned. Was there? Considering his reaction to Christy being on a date, he was afraid there was, but he'd be damned if he'd tell Jared that. "Nope."

Chapter 7

Christy was in her room, hiding from her boss who was not going to be happy when she found out both she and Fletch had left Bobby alone in the middle of the day.

The phone rang and she jumped. Since the phone was probably as old as the motel itself, there was no caller ID. But Mandy would probably call her cell, so Christy figured it was safe to answer.

"Hey there." Bobby's voice was warm and low, with not a hint of anger. It was the kind of voice that could make a woman melt. And for the moment, it was all for her.

Her heart fluttered. "Hi."

"I've got the late shift tonight. You wanna come with me?"

Mmm. If only that invitation were for her alone, but of course he meant Fletch, too. She didn't care. She was so relieved he wasn't mad any longer, she was willing to accept any tidbit he offered. Riding around in his car on a moonlit night was good enough, even if it was for work.

She swallowed and found her voice. "Sure."

"Good. I'll pick you up at your motel in an hour." She could hear his smile in his voice.

"OK."

He hung up and she scrambled off the bed and over to the closet. She pulled out the dress she'd worn the night before. It may have been wasted then, but it wouldn't be tonight. This evening, she'd wear it just for Bobby.

She was also looking forward to some good footage. The night shift, even on a slow night, seemed to be far more eventful than the day shift. Fletch could break out the night vision camera and they wouldn't miss a thing. Nighttime in Pigeon Hollow meant there was always a good share of drunken bar fights, and an even greater number of couples necking at the lover's lane by the river the moment the drive-in theater let out. Good TV.

None of that was different tonight, but it somehow

seemed like the winds had shifted. There was tension in the car, but it was no longer Bobby being uncomfortable in front of the camera. Oh, no. There seemed to be tension of an entirely different nature now.

It may have had something to do with the fact that Christy was sitting in the front seat next to Bobby while Fletch filmed from the back, a decree from Mandy now that Christy was a so-called character in the show. It may have also been that she knew Bobby had been jealous over her date with Corey, and that, sick as it was, gave her confidence. But Christy had a feeling it had even more to do with the fact that she had made up her mind. She was going after Bobby and it was going to be tonight. The minute Fletch was safely locked in his room, she was going to land Bobby, or go down trying.

There would be no more dilly-dallying. She had less than five weeks left with him and she wasn't going to waste any more of it.

She kept that resolve in mind when Bobby pulled up in front of The Hideaway. She turned to Fletch. "I need to plan the rest of this week's schedule with Bobby. I'll see you in the morning. OK?"

Fletch smiled and winked at her. "Sure, Christy. Night, Bobby."

"Night, Fletch."

The car door slammed and she turned in her seat to face him. And then she didn't know what to say.

He turned in his seat, too, and waited patiently, expectantly.

"Um. I...ah..." She let out a frustrated breath. This had gone so much better in her head.

He smiled. "You don't want to talk about the schedule, do you?"

She breathed with relief. "No."

"What do you wanna talk about?"

She hesitated, and then dove right in, which was really unlike her. "Maybe I don't want to talk at all."

He let out a breath of his own. "Ah, darlin'. I don't wanna talk either." Reaching out one hand, he stroked her face gently. She closed her eyes and enjoyed his touch.

She felt his hand cup the back of her head as he lowered his head toward hers. Her breath caught in her throat as their lips touched. She had imagined this moment so many times. The reality was immeasurably better.

With a groan, his tongue met hers. His mouth was warm and tasted like the coffee he'd been drinking that night. Tangling her hands in his hair, she leaned into him and kissed him until she was breathless.

She finally pulled back and asked, "Where can we go?"

He let out a short laugh. "We can't stay here, that's for sure. Not with half a dozen cameramen sleepin' inside."

She nodded. "What about by the river?"

He shook his head. "The next deputy on duty will be checkin' there hourly. They'll notice my car."

"Jared's hay room?" She suggested, not able to get that vision of rolling in the hay out of her head since Mandy suggested it.

He laughed. "Besides the fact we'd be trespassin', Jared's two hands both live in apartments up above the barn. And, hay isn't all it's cracked up to be."

Bobby let his hand trail down her back, sending a shiver up her spine. Letting out a sound of frustration, he pulled his hand away and turned back to the steering wheel. "I'm taking you back to my place."

Her mouth dropped open. "Your place meaning your parents' house. Where your parents and your sister and your nephew all live? Oh, no."

"Don't forget Cole, he's moved in now, too, since they got married. The new house won't be done for months."

"Have you lost your mind?" It was a serious question.

"No." He answered her just as seriously as he started the car and pulled out of the lot. "Look. You've been in my room. I'm way at the other end of the house and everyone in the family will have the air conditioners in their bedrooms

158

cranked up. No one will hear a thing."

"So you've done this before, I take it?" She wasn't sure how she felt about that. Actually, yes she was. She was jealous.

He grinned wickedly at her. "Not since I was about nineteen. But it worked then, it'll work now." He took his eyes off the road long enough to look at her. "You're jealous."

She pouted. "Yes."

He laughed. "She's married now with five kids and she's as big as a house. You have nothing to be jealous of."

"Well, after the way you treated me after one ice cream with Corey, maybe I have a right to be a little jealous. Huh?"

He nodded. "Yes, you do. I'm sorry about that. I was wrong."

She considered. "That's all right. If you hadn't been jealous, I think I would have been upset."

He laughed. "You would have, wouldn't you?"

"Yup."

He glanced at her again and reached out one hand to grab hers. "Why did I take so long to see what was right in front of me?"

"I don't know. Why did you?"

He squeezed her hand. "Because I'm a stubborn fool?"

Christy smiled. "Good answer."

They crept into the house like two thieves. Or, more accurately, like two overgrown teenagers who needed a place to have sex. While pausing every time a floorboard in the hall creaked, Bobby considered that he really needed to get his own place. It was long overdue. But until then, creep he would.

Halfway down the hall, Christy got the giggles and couldn't control them. Which made him get the giggles, too. If they didn't get to his room fast, they were going to get caught, and how embarrassing would that be. Briefly thinking that they should have brought a video camera with them so he could claim they were working—hey, it worked when he'd carry a book and tell his mother they were doing homework in his room—he grabbed Christy, flung her over his shoulder and ran for his door.

He dumped her in a giggling mass on top of the covers, closed his door and dove onto the bed next to her. And then there was no more laughing after the look she gave him. He leaned slowly towards her and she said on a shaky breath, "Oh, boy."

"You can say that again." She felt so good under his hands. He wasn't sure where he wanted to touch first. Barely able to think, he considered starting at the top and working his way down her gorgeous body. But her legs looked so great in the short little sundress she was wearing, he couldn't resist running a hand up her leg first.

At the same time, her hands were all over him, tugging the shirt of his uniform out of his pants. He didn't bother to unbutton it, but instead pulled it over his head, flung it to the floor and then went back to kissing her sweet mouth.

His hands made their way up her thighs, under the hem of the dress and over her panties until he reached her small waist. "I want you naked," he breathed in her ear, and then ran his tongue down her throat. She tasted slightly salty and he could have eaten her up.

She turned her head and glanced nervously at the bedroom door. "Does that door lock?"

He nodded and hopped off the bed to lock the door, anticipating what treats would await him afterwards. By the time he made it back to the bed, which was barely seconds, she was pulling the dress off over her head.

Hair tousled, lips swollen from kissing, and dressed in lingerie that amounted to two scraps of white lace, Christy was every man's wet dream. At least, she was his.

Hardly able to tear his gaze away from her, Bobby sat on the edge of the bed, pulled off his size twelve boots, unbuckled his belt and dropped his official deputy pants to the floor. Then a thought hit him.

"Shit." He scrambled across the queen-sized mattress

and reached for the nightstand. He pulled open the top drawer and rifled through the mess. Christy crawled her way across the bed and lay on her stomach next to him, peering around his shoulder.

"What's wrong?"

"I don't know if I have…phew. I do." He pulled out a single wrapped condom, what vintage he wasn't sure, but it would do. He'd stock up tomorrow. But at least tonight was taken care of. Maybe some more searching would yield a second, since he was certain that one time with Christy was not going to be enough for him. A whole lifetime with Christy probably wouldn't quench the desire he felt. That thought hit him pretty hard, but he decided to worry about it later.

She pulled herself up and glanced into the drawer, and then started laughing.

"What?"

She giggled. "Nothing. You're just such a man, I can't stand it."

"What do you mean?" He couldn't believe they were both in only their underwear and holding this conversation when they should be fucking, but something had amused her and now his interest was piqued.

"Look in that drawer! What's that?"

"A shot gun shell." He'd thrown it in there when he'd cleaned the gun and forgotten about it long ago.

She repeated his answer, laughing. "A shot gun shell, a half-eaten bag of corn chips and a condom. The contents of a manly-man's bedside table. I'm going to get that on film."

"Oh, no you're not." Then he smiled and grabbed her around the waist, pulling her on top of him. "You got a problem with manly-men?"

She shook her head and gazed down at him with moss colored eyes. "No. They are my favorite kind."

"Good." Then he decided that was enough of the nightstand discussion and kissed her again, plunging his tongue into her eager mouth.

Her mouth wasn't the only thing that was eager, and she reached her hands in between them, into his underwear and began stroking him.

He grabbed her hand and moved it away. "Nuh, uh." If she kept that up, they wouldn't need the condom at all, he'd spew before he even got inside her.

She pulled her hand out of his, nibbled on his lip and reached right back down to grasp him again.

Capturing the hand again, he rolled them both over and held both of her hands over her head. "You are a stubborn little devil, aren't you?"

Her smile was both sweet and evil at the same time as she nodded and tried to free her hands from his grasp.

His eyes opened wide at her in warning. "Christy. I'm barely hanging on by the skin of my teeth as it is. Stop grabbing me."

"OK. I'll be good."

Trusting her, he released her hands, leaving his free to explore her gorgeous body more. He'd just released one of her perfect breasts from its lacy confines when he felt her hand snake its way into his underwear and start exploring. Just that touch sent a tremor through him.

There was no possible way he could concentrate on enjoying her body with her hands teasing him like that. Shaking his head at her, he reached down to his pants on the floor, grabbed his handcuffs and, before she realized what he was doing, had both of her hands over her head and cuffed to the headboard.

Her eyes opened wide.

"I warned you and you promised to be good." He was about to tell her he'd release her if she promised and actually behaved herself this time when her expression changed.

Her eyes lost focus and her breathing started to come faster. Suddenly the realization hit him that she liked being handcuffed. Looking at her like that, he realized he was breathing harder himself. He swallowed. "Christy, this is really..."

162

She finished his sentence shakily. "…a turn on?"

He nodded. "Oh, yeah." Running his hands down her constrained body, he asked, practically begged, actually, "Can you stay like this, just for bit?"

Her eyes drifted all the way closed and she nodded. "Mmm, hmm."

He slid down her body and began what he'd been dying to do for probably longer than he even realized. Pulling down her panties, he explored her folds with his fingers as his mouth found her breast.

She groaned and arched her back beneath him. He groaned himself and suckled harder while his fingers plunged deeper.

She writhed on the bed beneath him and he heard the chains of the cuffs rubbing against the wooden headboard. Forcing himself back to reality for a moment, he asked. "You all right?"

Taking a shaky breath, she answered. "Oh, yeah."

"Good." He couldn't have been happier to hear that as he slid lower and spread her legs wide. His mouth found the spot he knew would drive her crazy and he felt her shudder. He worked harder with both mouth and hands and she cried out above him.

Somewhere through the sex-induced haze, he realized his entire family was sleeping nearby. He reached up and slapped one hand over her mouth as he brought her to a powerful orgasm. She strained against the cuffs and his hand, but he didn't remove it as she moaned loudly.

He was going to find someplace private to take her, and *take* her, tomorrow. He didn't care if they had to sneak away from the cameras, drive fifty miles and check into a hotel, next time he was going to hear her full volume and enjoy every moment of it.

When she finally stilled beneath him, he raised himself off her, found the condom again and crawled up her body.

With her legs spread wide, she was more than ready for him and he was about to plunge himself into her when he found himself eyelevel with the handcuffs. He glanced down at her and the question must have shown on his face.

Christy shook her head. "I'm OK."

He breathed out, relieved. "Thank you." Then he slid home with a shudder and held himself deep.

She raised her hips off the bed, unable to do much more with her hands still above her head. Afraid to move much until he calmed himself down, he nudged gently into her, enjoying the warmth and really enjoying the little gasps each small thrust produced from Christy.

"Oh, Bobby. Keep doing that. I'm going to..." Her sentence trailed off as her breath came in gasps and he felt her shatter around him as she came again.

He covered her mouth with his and matched the rhythm of her spasms with his own thrusts until he exploded within her. It was a good thing his mouth was over hers because he thought he was probably pretty loud himself.

Exhausted, he wanted nothing more than to collapse next to her, but he realized he needed to find the key, no matter how shaky his arms were at the moment. He managed to reach his pants on the floor without taking a header off the bed, locate the key and uncuff her hands from the headboard.

She looped shaky arms around his neck and sighed. "That was the most incredible sex I've ever experienced."

Smiling, he had to agree.

Looking a little hesitant, she asked him, "You've never...I mean, have you ever? You know, done that before?"

He shook his head and reassured her, laughing. "No. I never thought I was into that kind of stuff. But it was really hot, wasn't it?"

"Yeah, it was. Does that make us perverts?"

He cringed. "I don't think I'll be tellin' the pastor about it any time soon, but it's not like we did anythin' really bad."

For the first time he noticed her wrists were rubbed red from the cuffs. He touched the marks gently. "You sure you're all right?"

"I'm fine. I swear. But next time, it's your turn." Christy wore a devilish look and ran one finger down his chest, all the way to his groin.

He opened his eyes wide. "I don't know about that." That was all he needed, to have someone hear he'd been cuffed to a bed with his own handcuffs!

Eyes narrowed, she said, "We'll see." Visions of what her sexy mouth and her soft hands could do to him filled his head and his resolve crumbled.

He cupped her face and smiled playfully, knowing he'd give in to her. "We'll see."

Chapter 8

Christy glanced around the room she had called home for the past eight weeks nostalgically. It wasn't so much that she would miss the room itself, with its lack of hot water and authentic 1950's décor. But the memories she'd made while staying there for the last two months would stay with her for the rest of her life.

Mandy knocked on the frame of the open door. "Time to go."

Christy smiled at her once hated boss and surprised herself by tearing up.

Mandy smiled back as her own eyes welled with unshed tears. She sniffed loudly and laughed. "Don't you start or I will to."

Christy nodded and then laughed as the tears fell freely anyway. "I'm going to miss you."

Mandy stepped forward and pulled her into a hug. "I'll miss you, too. Are you sure?"

Christy nodded. "Quite sure."

Mandy shrugged. "Can't blame me for trying to keep you with me. You are not only one of the best associate producers I've ever worked with, you're also my friend."

That sentence twisted the knot already lodged firmly in Christy's belly and her resolve wavered briefly. "Thank you. That means a lot to me."

Mandy released her and wiped at her eyes. "Can't let Jared see me crying. He'll think it's over him and won't let me go."

"And it's not over him?"

Mandy hesitated a beat. "I'm going to tell you something, as a friend, not as your boss, and you have to keep it totally quiet."

"OK."

Mandy smiled. "I'm going back to LA and I'm going to make sure this is the highest-rated damn reality series on the air. And then, after I collect the Emmy Award, I'm quitting."

Christy gasped.

Mandy nodded and continued. "I've got a call into a head hunter who deals with the entire south-eastern US. She's sure she can find me a job on my own terms, and at least then Jared and I will be on the same side of country."

"Does he know?"

"Yeah. Of course he'd be happiest with me moved to the farm and baking pies with Lois, but I'm not sure I'm quite ready for that yet. I don't know. We'll see. Although, if he keeps trying to convince me in the creative ways he's been coming up with lately, I might just change my mind. And if I have an Emmy award to stand on that big old mantle in the Gordon living room, I might really change my mind." Mandy smiled.

Christy grabbed Mandy's hands and squeezed them. Over the last two months, they'd actually become friends. "Well, whether you're in the Gordon house baking pies or not, I'll be glad when we're on the same side of the country, too."

A large shadow blocked the sun streaming in through the open doorway and announced Bobby's arrival. She heard his deep voice. "All packed?"

Christy dried her eyes quickly and tilted her head toward the two suitcases, zipped and standing on the floor. "All packed."

Bobby stepped inside. "Hey, Mandy. Jared was just pulling up behind me."

"Thanks, Bobby." Mandy smiled one last time at Christy. "You better call and email me whenever you can. OK?"

Christy nodded and then Mandy left and she was alone with Bobby.

His thumb brushed the side of her face. "You all right?"

She leaned her face into his hand and enjoyed the warm feel of him. "Yeah. It's just starting to hit that as of today, I'm unemployed." She'd thought she hated her job, but now that she didn't have it anymore, she was thinking maybe it hadn't been that bad after all. Wasn't that always the way?

Bobby pursed his lips and drew her into his arms. "I'm sorry for how you're feelin', but I'm not sorry that I'm glad you're stayin', unemployed or not."

She buried her head in his chest. "I'm not sorry I'm staying, either."

Pulling back, he looked down at her. "I know you've grown fond of The Hideaway for some strange reason, but are you ready to move into your new home now?"

She smacked his arm playfully. "Hey, we've made some good memories here!" Once they realized they weren't fooling anyone by sneaking around, they'd given up hiding and Bobby started to just spend nights there with her. It was far preferable to having sex under his parents' roof.

Bobby glanced at the bed and smiled. "Yes, we have. But it's time to christen our new bedroom."

She laughed. "Are you sure you soundproofed the walls of that apartment above your parents' garage?"

"Oh, yeah. Double thick insulation and three-quarter inch sheetrock, brand new double pane windows and a very loud air-conditioning unit." He lowered his mouth to within a breath of hers. "You can be as loud as you want."

"And so can you," she teased, grabbing his butt.

He smiled. "You do what you did to me last night and I'll be real loud."

She raised herself up on tiptoe and kissed him.

The stuff from her apartment that her roommate had packed and shipped might not be arriving for another week, but Bobby was here now. And that was all she really needed to make Pigeon Hollow her home.

Epilogue

TV Weekly Magazine

Smalltown, USA Wrap-up

Smalltown, USA, the surprise hit reality show that took the country by storm, wrapped up its season with a bang Sunday night when Producer Mandy Morris took home the Emmy Award for best prime-time reality television series. Morris verified the rumor that she is leaving the production company responsible for the show to 'pursue personal interests'. Being that *Smalltown* star Jared Gordon was her date for the event, TV Weekly wonders if her personal business may lie back in Pigeon Hollow, where the show was filmed.

It is not surprising the series won the hearts and ratings of America with its flawless editing and a cast of characters that would make any producer drool. Handsome horseman Jared Gordon, his red-hot, pie-baking mama Lois, Mac the gruff but lovable diner owner, Sue Ann, the villain everyone loved to hate (who was reportedly last seen headlining at Naughty Ladies strip club in Atlanta) were all household names by the end of the run.

Ratings soared during the revelation of the unexpected romance that blossomed between Deputy Sheriff Bobby Barton and Associate Producer Christy Dunne, only to be surpassed by the revelation of ex-major league pitcher Cole Ryan's love child and the ensuing reunion with former love Lizzie Barton.

Industry analysts speculate that the success of *Smalltown* will spur an influx of copycat shows by next season, leaving this reporter to wonder if any other cast will ever be able to fill the shoes of the people of Pigeon Hollow.

The End

About the Author:

It all started in first grade when Cat Johnson won the essay contest at Hawthorne Elementary School and got to ride in the Chief of Police's car in the Memorial Day Parade...and the rest, as they say, is history. As an adult, Cat generally tries to stay out of police cars and is thrilled to be writing for a living. She has been published under a different name in the Young Adult genre, but Linden Bay is the first to release her romances.

On a personal note, Cat has two horses, 10 cats, one dog, six parakeets, numerous fish and one husband, and is not sure which of those gives her the most grief. Needless to say, she is very busy most days on her little 18th century farm in New York State. She plays the harp professionally and stresses that this does not mean she plays well. A past bartender, marketing manager and Junior League president, Cat's life is quite the dichotomy, and on any given day she is just as likely to be in formal eveningwear as in mucking clothes covered in manure. Cat hates the telephone but loves email, and is looking forward to hearing from you.

cat.johnson@lindenbayromance.com

Other works by Cat Johnson:

Trilogy No. 102: Opposites Attract

...a three-part lighthearted romp through the intertwining lives of six people who learn that in spite of everything you have to remember to live, love and laugh to be happy.

Taking a Leap: Bradley Morgan is the quintessential computer geek and nice guy, through and through. The only problem is that in his opinion, nice guys almost always finish last when it comes to hot women like his sexy co-worker Alyssa Jones. But things change after Alyssa finds her boyfriend cheating. Suddenly, nice guys like Brad don't look so bad. So when Brad agrees to ghostwrite the sex scenes for a romance novel as a favor for desperate client Maria White and asks for Alyssa's help after hours, she agrees wholeheartedly and things really start to heat up. Brad and Alyssa learn you should never judge a book by its cover, and that sometimes love requires a leap of faith.

Light my Fire: Amy Gerald's life is filled with whirlwind romance. Unfortunately, it's all on the pages of the romance novels she publishes. That is until she volunteers to cat-sit for her author friend Maria and meets Troy O'Donnell, the hunky fireman who lives next door. The problem is, this commitment-phobic consummate bachelor is far more willing to run into a burning building than allow love into his life. Troy will grasp at any excuse, even the ridiculous assumption that Amy is a lesbian, just to avoid his growing feelings for her. Amid a comedy of errors and misunderstandings, which includes Troy's first hilarious visit to a gay bar, Amy manages to light Troy's fire, but can she also conquer his fears?

Second Time Around: Antonio Sanchez thought that at 32 his life was all mapped out--wife, kids, career...until some major bumps in the road radically alter his course and send him careening right into the path of newly divorced Maddie Morgan. Suddenly thrust back into single life, Antonio moves back in with his old-fashioned parents and has to learn to juggle his kids, his job at the firehouse, and his role as Best Man for his newly engaged best friend Troy, all in addition to facing his unquenchable desire for Maddie. Throw in a slew of matchmaking friends and relatives, led by Maria whose apartment appears to be the Bermuda Triangle for lost lovers, and Antonio and Maddie discover just how complicated things can get. Can the pair prove that love really is better the second time around?

Trilogy No. 103: Red Hot & Blue

Trey: Special operative Trey Williams doesn't want a girlfriend, nor does he need one in his life. A distracted soldier is a dead soldier, that's his motto. The problem is, the woman who has been recruited to pose as his wife on a special assignment is proving to be more of a distraction than Trey can handle. What's a soldier to do?

Jack: Ordered by his superiors to take time off for his "mental health", Jack Gordon heads back to his hometown for two weeks of R&R. But then he meets Nicki Camp, the new hand his brother has just hired to help out at the family farm. Is Nicki playing hard to get, or is she hiding something? Jack knows one thing…he isn't going to rest until he finds out!

Jimmy: Jimmy Gordon has learned during his career in the Special Forces that he can handle pretty much anything, including pretending to be everything from a banquet waiter to a terrorist, while undercover. But there is one thing he finds he's having a bit of difficulty handling, and that's the governor's hot red-headed daughter, Amelia Monroe-Carrington. Maybe the time for pretending is over?

This is a publication of
Linden Bay Romance
WWW.LINDENBAYROMANCE.COM

Recommended Linden Bay Romance Read:

Trilogy No. 101: Turning Up The Heat

You just never know where you're going to find love....

Blackout: Ashley and Curt get trapped together in an elevator. As the temperature rises they begin to reveal themselves in more ways then one!

Touch the Fire: Firefighter Garrett Flint rescues the beautiful Nicole from a burning building and then breaks all the rules by taking her into his home and into his heart.

June in August: June Monroe grew up next door to Wiley Patton. When he left for Vietnam she was just fifteen and hopelessly in love. Now three years later he's returned from war and little June is all grown up.

623995

Made in the USA